CW01099431

Memoirs of the Messed Up Minds

Memoirs of the Messed Up Minds

Brandon Wilkinson

iUniverse, Inc.
New York Lincoln Shanghai

Memoirs of the Messed Up Minds

Copyright © 2007 by Brandon Wilkinson

All rights reserved. No part of this book may be used or reproduced by any means, graphic, electronic, or mechanical, including photocopying, recording, taping or by any information storage retrieval system without the written permission of the publisher except in the case of brief quotations embodied in critical articles and reviews.

iUniverse books may be ordered through booksellers or by contacting:

iUniverse
2021 Pine Lake Road, Suite 100
Lincoln, NE 68512
www.iuniverse.com
1-800-Authors (1-800-288-4677)

This is a work of fiction. All of the characters, names, incidents, organizations, and dialogue in this novel are either the products of the author's imagination or are used fictitiously.

ISBN-13: 978-0-595-42986-8 (pbk)
ISBN-13: 978-0-595-87327-2 (ebk)
ISBN-10: 0-595-42986-6 (pbk)
ISBN-10: 0-595-87327-8 (ebk)

Printed in the United States of America

ACKNOWLEDGMENTS

Each of the following stories takes an unusual look into the human psyche, leading to a variety of twists and turns along the way, as well as unexpected conclusions. The subject matter is edgy throughout, often dark, but scattered with a comedic element from beginning to end.

Definitely not intended for a juvenile audience, and there's never any danger I'll be invited to do a recital at a kiddies party. There is an element of profanity and other adult content, which I fully attribute to my Scottish upbringing and friends—it was unavoidable!

I'm sure you'll enjoy reading these tales as much as I did writing them. I had a blast, and encountered a multitude of emotions all the way through.

Without the encouragement from my wife Teri, John my Dad, Betty my Mum, and my not so "wee" brother Alan, the following pages would currently be gathering dust in a closet somewhere.

I'd also like to give a huge thanks to my friends. Not only those from Scotland, but those in the United States also, some American born and bred, the others also transplants from my side of the pond. Without you all, the inspiration from your wit, and our time spent with a Guinness in our hands telling weird and wonderful stories, there would've been no foundation for my ideas.

<u>My Scottish Inspirational Friends</u>:
Big Graeme, Chris, Scotty Boy, John Harvey, Stevie, Deery and my big 'cuz' Calum.
The best group of guys you could ever meet, and I miss you all greatly.

<u>The American Lads</u> (including the Irish, Welsh & English transplants)
Dec, Robbie, John P, Conrad, Don and Perry.

Both groups of guys have given me fond, not to mention wild memories that will undoubtedly influence my future work.

Come Fly with Me

<u>Come Fly with Me</u>

1

Bitch and Bobble Head

"We're sorry Calum, but we're going to have to let you go."

The words pulsated in my head like the beat from my pounding heart. I'd never been fired before. The words "let go" were such bullshit—a candy coated version attempting to make you feel better about the situation. The only ones feeling better with this verbage were the assholes in front of me right now, the ones keeping their jobs.

"Yes, I can tell you're feeling bad about it," I said in my smuggest of tones.

"Well thank you Calum for your understanding. You'd be amazed at the attitudes of some of the others," said Elizabeth Hunter, the overweight and generally grotesque head of Human Resources. Her sidekick Nancy, nodding in agreement like the little butt kissing puppet that she was. I thought my sarcastic retort was as obvious as a pygmy in a basketball game, but apparently not. Their lack of intellectual interpretation almost caused a snigger, but I compressed it to a minor grin.

"I must say Calum, your upbeat demeanor really is refreshing. I'm sure it will hold you in good stead for your future pursuits." Again Nancy the retard agreed in predictable fashion. She could have doubled as a fucking bobble head. Perhaps if she was ever "let go" that would be a career path worth exploring.

Reality suddenly kicked in, and this could not have occurred at a worse moment. Everyone in the company knew lays off were coming, but just not sure who or how many. No doubt my recent personal problems had played a part in my dismissal. Regular sick days, late arrival and a drop in performance had been the by-product of my failing marriage.

I was in a world of my own as I packed up what little belongings I had, throwing in some extra company stationary just out of spite. What would I do now? The severance package equated to a Saturday afternoon spending spree at Macy's by my soon to be ex-wife. It wasn't official, but in my mind, divorce was inevitable and likely to cost me considerably.

"We're going to miss you Calum," said a faint high-pitched voice.

I turned to see Rachel, our department secretary, with a sad look on her face and her eyes looking very glassy.

"Now now Rachel, it's not that bad. I was looking for a way out anyway. Finally going to get a chance to start the home business I've been thinking about for a while." My upbeat response seemed to alter her appearance. If only I had believed my façade.

"We're all still sad to see you go Calum. Things won't be the same here without you".

"Life goes on though. You safe for now?" I asked quizzically.

"I think so. They haven't said anything to me so I assume so. You never know with this place though."

"I'm sure you'll be fine. Carter won't be able to function without you coordinating his daily schedule." Leonard Carter was the department boss. A useless, middle-aged guy with the organizational skills of the three stooges on crack.

"Anyway, the team wanted to see if you could meet us for a few drinks tonight. Nothing fancy, just a little get together in town as a send off for you."

"Sounds good, I could use a few drinks that's for sure."

"Eight o'clock at the Tiger Bar sound OK for you?"

"That works for me. Keep your chin up Rachel, it really is alright. There's a lot of people in this world much worse off than me you know."

"I know, but it still doesn't make it right. You're a good man Calum."

She was very sincere, which was extremely touching. Rachel was aware I was having a few relationship issues and I could tell she thought it was not my fault.

"Anyway, I'd better get on my way before I'm physically removed. I'll see you tonight." I gave her a wink and she responded with a smile and a hug.

This Company didn't mess around. No sooner had I walked away from Rachel but I spotted Bitch and Bobble Head waiting to escort me off the premises. With them was a sour faced cop wannabe security guard, who obviously believed he had as much power as the Company CEO. What was it about uniforms that turned people into complete dicks? I felt like a convict being led to the gas chamber as I walked with Laurel and Hardy of the Human Resources world, closely followed by Lieutenant Minimum Wage of our elite special forces Security team! The Bitch was attempting to engage me in some form of idle chit chat as we walked, but I was oblivious to it all—just grunting in agreement every time Bobble Head wobbled her neck like Jay Leno on his late night show.

I climbed into the driver's seat of the car and closed the door firmly behind me.

"Fuck, fuck, fuck." I was like Hugh Grant in the opening scene of Four Weddings and a Funeral, realizing I'd overslept for the big day. What the hell was I going to do? Things at home were bad enough right now without throwing another variable into the equation. My overall frame of mind was as fragile as Nicole Ritchie's forearm, and I was in no mental state to go through the whole job interview process over again. Shit, I couldn't even keep myself together for the one I'd just lost. I was just glad I'd decided against taking the company car option, going instead for the five thousand extra on the annual salary. I would've been really screwed then, stranded here in the parking lot, having to call her to come and pick me up. Then she would have known. Perhaps I wouldn't tell her and try to find something new before the lack of money kicked in. Who knew what to do? One thing was for sure, I didn't. The only thing for certain was that I was looking forward to a drink this evening.

2

Marital Bliss

I arrived home to the sound I'd been hoping for—silence. My wife Jennifer was likely still working. Regardless of what she was doing, the main thing was that she wasn't here. Her work hours varied substantially. She was a realtor and the current market was going through quite a lull, which was even more of a reason for today's bad timing.

We'd been married now for just over two years. Like most marriages, the first six months had been great. She had the sex drive of a porn star and we made love around five times a week. Sometimes the weekends were like a sexathon, exploring different positions and rooms in the house—what more could a man ask for. Then things started to slow down. My job was getting very stressful and often she was showing houses at night. Our time together began to get less and less and sex seemed like a special occasion. This rut continued for around a year and developed into our normal operating procedure. We were growing apart and our love for each other was diminishing by the day. Arguments over trivial matters seemed to blow up into full-scale major issues and nights spent sleeping on the couch were on the increase.

The shit hit the fan two months ago when I moved into the spare bedroom. Apparently my snoring was the issue, but it was likely just another smoke screen to drive our pathetic relationship further apart.

"Maybe I should move into the other room permanently."

"Maybe you should, you're always on the couch anyway, continuously making the same lame ass excuse that you accidentally fell asleep while watching TV. Then when you bother to bring yourself back to bed, your breathing sounds like an earthquake that's hit a record high on the Richter scale."

She really was a smart ass, which I *used* to find cute. It was the following day that I moved my clothes and other useless bits and pieces into the spare room. The only positive from it was I realized how little pieces of clothing I actually owned, as well as how deprived I was in the footwear department—I really needed to go shopping. There was never any room in our joint closets, but my entire belongings hung in the spare room like the pathetic leftover items from an all day Macy's clearance sale.

Snoring, what a cheek, nothing compared to her farting in her sleep. I should have brought that one up, but we were already going tit for tat like a couple of whiny school kids. She had a point though with my sleeping on the couch, but I'd never own up to anything. There were a few occasions that I'd genuinely fallen asleep during a movie or something, but I'd become comfortable with my own company. It was peaceful and argument free, not to mention the added luxury of being able to masturbate with some passion, as opposed to carrying out the act with her lying next to me, suspecting she was asleep, but never 100% sure. That was never a good jerking session, stroking myself with the deliberateness of a bomb disposal expert diffusing a deadly device. Jennifer wasn't really giving me any pleasure to speak of anymore, so the sessions on my own had become important to me. I needed to able to move around a little, really get into it, throw in a few grunts and groans, not to mention a sporadic curse word under my breath as I envisioned banging it like a wild animal into a grateful and overly satisfied Pamela Anderson.

Yeah, it was just easier to sleep apart. It wasn't like there would be any more success in the sex department if we were sharing a mattress. Shit, we were hardly sharing a conversation right now never mind bodily fluids. Neither of us complained as we began our separate lives under the same roof, and as with all our other diminishing activities, this quickly turned into the norm without any further debate.

3

Beer

It was approaching seven o'clock and no sign of Jennifer. I was relieved in a way as it was delaying the bad news I had in store. Not that it seemed to matter. Our lives had become so detached, it seemed that divorce was just around the corner. We hadn't had sex in over three months now. Even the last time had felt like we were just going through the motions. We'd had a few drinks and ended up having a quick one. There was no passion, no excitement and the climax was anything but.

I had my suspicions. There was no way a woman with her drive wasn't up to something. Either she was going through Duracell batteries like they were going out of fashion or she was having something on the side. I hoped and prayed it wasn't the latter. I could never cheat on her. I took my marriage vows very seriously. Maybe we could get it back to the ways of old—perhaps a vacation to the Bahamas. Get the old honeymoon juices flowing again. I should have tried more, but my stubbornness always got the better of me. We were like apples and apples in that way—neither of us giving in. The more I thought of her having an affair the more it was getting me down. Where was she? The housing market was in the toilet bowl right now. There was no way she was still working, was there? Come on Calum, get your shit together, no time to be getting all down on yourself.

I called a cab to take me to the bar. I waited intently in the living room, periodically watching Sports Center in between contemplating my diminishing marriage.

A set of headlights pulled into the driveway—she was finally back. I pulled back the curtain only to see the familiar sign on top of the waiting taxi. I gave the driver an almost lifeless acknowledgment.

It was Friday night and the town was bustling. Jazz style music oozed from the doorway as I eased past the bouncer, greeting him with a fake smile. It only seemed like yesterday that I was regularly asked for I.D entering such an establishment. I was only thirty, but the last couple of years had taken their toll on me. My boyish looks had been replaced by a few grey hairs and minor wrinkles around the eyes. I looked around the bar, a nice looking place with a cozy feel to it. The music as I entered had given the perception that it was packed, but it was anything but. It wasn't even eight o'clock though and things didn't usually pick up until around ten.

"Calum."

I looked over to the far corner by the restrooms to see Rachel waving at me. I got the impression she would be on time. Organized and punctual could've been her middle name. She looked quite striking, almost resembling a thinner version of Minnie Driver, all glammed up and her long dark hair was down— she was immaculate and genuinely pleased to see me. It seemed not so long ago that Jennifer made the same type of effort.

"How you holding up Calum," said David.

"Pretty good. I'll be doing a lot better when I get a cold one down my throat."

David was a good guy, a stocky little fellow with a receding hairline and shiny red cheeks. The brightness of his face matched his cheerful nature. He was another one who was punctual by nature—never late for a days work in his life and this obviously carried over to social events. Most people these days believed in being fashionably late, as they liked to call it. If you said eight o'clock, you could bet they would arrive some time after eight thirty. That was always something that had puzzled me. Why did people not like to be the first ones to arrive at a social event? Perhaps it was the fear of getting there and potentially having to make idle chit chat with someone they didn't really like, probably more in their comfort zone when there's already a group there, less pressure to be entertaining or something. What did I know?

"I hear you Calum. That first one went down a treat. What you having?"

"I'll take a Guinness if they have it."

"Good man Calum, a real beer drinker. Never understood these guys and their light beers, they may as well be drinking a soda. How you doing on yours Rachel?"

"I'm fine for now David."

The waitress wasn't around, so David made his way to the bar.

"How did Jennifer take the news?" said Rachel with a hint of anguish.

"Didn't tell her yet. I was thinking about it, but she still wasn't home when I left."

"You sound like things are pretty messed up."

"That's an understatement. I think it's just a matter of time to be honest with you. There's just no spark anymore. I've even got my suspicions she's having an affair."

I had no idea why I'd shared those thoughts. Rachel was just so easy to talk to and seemed genuinely concerned, and I was sure she wouldn't share this with the others. She didn't seem the type. My life was so empty right now and it was nice being able to talk to someone of the opposite sex.

"Oh Calum, I really am sorry," she said resting her hand on top of mine.

"Not to worry. Anyway, this is a night out. Let's not kill the mood with my problems. Tonight is a time for drinking to the future and good times. How's your love life?"

"Great—not seeing anyone at the moment. I need a break from complications right now, but I'm loving every minute of it."

"Good to hear. Wish I could change shoes with you right now." I gave her a wink and a grin and she reciprocated.

"One pint of Guinness Calum. One of many tonight no doubt," said David giving me a hearty pat on the back.

I'd never been drinking with David before, but from the sounds of it he was really into his beer. He too was married and maybe wanted to make the most of his night of freedom.

"You can bet your balls on that David. Sorry Rachel, didn't mean to be crude in front of a lady."

"Lady? There's no lady at this table tonight. I might seem all prim and proper at the office, but I've got a mouth like a Sailor—you can bet your balls on that."

The three of us laughed and the overall mood gradually elevated. I was having a great time. We had another couple of drinks and my worries were evaporating like a puddle on a warm Summer's day.

Finally another few people arrived. Like I thought, fashionably forty five minutes late. Our account manager Jeff, Mark our Customer liaison and Pamela our Quality lead. All nice folk and I was happy they'd made the effort to come out. Jeff was a fairly quiet guy, but had a really dry sense of humor. Mark was anything but quiet. Being our key Customer contact, he was outgoing and used to making presentations in front of crowded rooms as well as being highly experienced in negotiation. He had the gift of the gab and was a real hoot. As the night progressed he only got funnier. Even Pamela was coming out of her shell. She was occasionally referred to as the Librarian, in light of the way she wore her hair in a bun, and the slender framed glasses that often appeared perched on the end of her nose, almost defying gravity. It was amazing what a few drinks and getting away from the political correctness of corporate life could do. It looked like Mark and Pamela were a little more than friends. I noticed a few shared glances and they were very touchy feely. Again it caused me flashbacks to the marriage I once had—I needed another beer.

It really was fascinating what alcohol could do. We all knew each other, but not really on a personal basis—maybe with the exception of Mark and Pamela. Their initial discreetness had been replaced by hand holding and was only verified when the subject of conversation stumbled onto favorite sexual positions. In her drunken state, Pamela stated that she liked it from behind.

"He really gets it in deep doing it doggy style," she said looking into Mark's eyes and giving his arm a squeeze for us all to see. As soon as she'd blurted it out, she realized she'd screwed up and apologized to Mark immediately, which only confirmed their intimate status and added fuel to the fire for our light hearted teasing.

"So you like it from behind Pamela. Does Mark enjoy it also?" I asked inquisitively.

"He's had no complaints so far, have you Mark".

"So Mark likes it from behind? What a kinky bastard," I said, before Mark had a chance to reply to her.

"Oh my God, not like that. He likes giving it from behind," said Pamela in shock.

"I'm not so sure about that, looks like a bit of a sausage smuggler if you ask me," piped in David, trying to hold in his laughter as Pamela continued to fret.

"I can assure you he's one hundred percent heterosexual. In fact, that's why we were late this evening. He was giving me a good …"

"It's OK honey," interrupted Mark quickly. "They're just messing with you."

The entire table erupted in drunken laughter as Pamela realized how gullible she'd been. We gave a toast to "Mark and Pamela" followed by a miniature cheer and continued around the table for more favorite positions. It was David next, but I didn't really catch what he was saying as I was distracted by the feel of a hand on the inside of my right knee. Maybe it was all this sex talk and the accumulation of alcohol, but it was coming from Rachel. I glimpsed briefly into her eyes. She returned a seductive grin and simultaneously squeezed my leg again. Surprised I was, bothered I wasn't. In fact it was rather nice, and between the conversation topic and my lack of recent sexual activity, I was beginning to get aroused. Rachel squeezed again and this time I returned a little smile. I glanced around the table, but nobody had noticed. They were way too into the topic of discussion. No doubt this would be the part of the evening that David and Jeff would conveniently forget to tell their wives about.

Rachel's wandering hand continued in a Northern direction, much to my excitement.

"So what about you Rachel," asked Mark.

All eyes were in Rachel's direction now, so I did my best not to move. Her hand was now planted on my groin. I prayed I didn't suddenly need the bathroom. I was pitching a little gnome tent down there right now and would need some time to shake this off.

"I like to take control of my man. Some women like to be dominated, but I like to be on top. Nobody knows what I want more than I do."

No kidding—her fingers were slowly rubbing my package.

"Wow, think a cold shower for me would be a good idea right now," chuckled David.

"Tell me about it. Not sure I can handle this excitement for much longer," winked Jeff.

"Might be too late for me," laughed Mark.

That was a great line, and wasn't far from my current scenario. I hadn't jerked off in several days, so I was a prime candidate for a premature finish. Nevertheless, she continued the inconspicuous massage and I was glad.

"Last but not least. What about you Calum?" asked Rachel with an extra rub.

"I actually have to agree with you Rachel. I like my women on top. So they can control the depth and angles and stuff. There's also the fact I'm a bit of a lazy bastard."

What a great night, the relaxed nature of it all was really helping me, and everyone was in a fantastic mood. These guys were even cooler than I'd thought. As for Rachel, what a surprise she'd turned out to be. She was attractive and getting hotter after each beer and every stroke of her magician like fingers, but I just couldn't cheat on Jennifer. What if I was wrong about her affair? I would feel like a complete dick if I was and had just screwed another woman. Not sure I could deal with the guilt. In my head though, what was going on at the table right now was acceptable. I had initiated nothing and wasn't saying anything to stop the proceedings, as I didn't want to cause a scene. That was the logic in my head and I was sticking to it—right or wrong.

We drank for another hour or so before calling it a night. By now I was really feeling the affects and my vision was a little blurred. Mark and Jeff were physically helping Pamela out of the front door. They wished me luck and climbed into a waiting cab. David and Rachel lived near one another and had planned to share a taxi home.

"Calum, it's been a pleasure, we should do this again sometime. Please stay in touch," said David.

He was a nice guy and I was sure I'd take him up on the beer offer at some point.

Rachel gave me a hug and whispered in my ear.

"You can come home with me if you'd like?"

"I'd love to, but I can't, not right now. I know where to find you if I need to talk. Thanks again for a great night."

I was sincere about that, but left her with a cute little wink—no harm in some flirting. I grabbed the cab parked behind theirs, gave some slurred directions to the driver and sank slowly into a semi-conscious state.

4

Come Fly with Me

I was back in my living room, but didn't remember getting out of the cab, or the entire ride home for that matter. This was the drunkest I'd been since my wedding. Think the fresh air after leaving the bar had really caused the beer to move into overdrive. Jennifer was home. I could hear her gentle little snores and occasional fart as I listened carefully at her bedroom door. It would've been easier to look in the driveway for her car, but a clear thought process was not at the forefront right now. I did have the sense to at least let her sleep. I staggered back to my room and climbed into bed. What'd happened to my life? What a mess. Where was it headed? These thoughts pounded my skull as I gradually passed out.

I flew like a super hero through the valley, piercing the wind like a bullet. The birds seemed to know I was like one of them now. They formed a V-shape behind me. It was almost like they knew I was the Captain of the ship. The village below was crowded. The people were like little ants going about their daily lives. I swooned down for a closer look. My new found feathered friends did not follow. It was like they knew something was amiss. They circled overhead as I closed in on the life below. As I neared the scene, a young schoolgirl was contented as she slurped on her ice-cream cone, oblivious to the tragedy that lay ahead.

The truck driver sped around the winding road, occasional weaving across the median. I sensed he was new to the area. My vision honed in on his almighty cab window. Map in hand, he continued on, only partial attention on the road ahead. As she stepped out on the village street, the shrieking of brakes were almost drowned out by her screaming Mother. My friends above squabbled with anguish, sensing the immediate doom. I dived like a swallow, not a minute too soon, sweeping her into my arms and out of harms way. The ice-cream cone was not as lucky.

"Thank God Calum," sobbed the distraught Mother.

"All in a days work Madam."

"I don't know what we'd do without you."

"Now young lady, take care on the road in future. Look left, look right and only cross if it's all clear, you hear me?"

She nodded contently, but had no idea of her near death experience. I was convinced she was more upset about the loss of the ice-cream. I leaped back into the air. My friends chirping ecstatically with applause, as the V-formation was reunited and we headed on our way.

I was awakened by the sound of the kettle whistling. Surprisingly my head was clear and I felt as calm and relaxed as I had in a long time. What a crazy dream. It felt so life like though. The feeling of flying was exhilarating—like nothing I'd experienced before. I wasn't really one for dreaming, but that was unbelievable. I felt so alive. I got up and headed through to the kitchen where Jennifer was making herself a cup of coffee.

"Got one for me?" I inquired.

"Sure. Take it you need one this morning. Late night was it?"

"Yeah, went out for a couple of drinks with a few people from the office. I waited around for you, but had to leave around seven or so. Working late were you?"

"Was showing a couple of houses," she said, using her fingers to brush her hair over her ears. This wasn't a good signal. Anytime she lied, this was a tell tale sign. She couldn't lie for shit and would never make a poker player.

"Manage to close any deals?"

"Don't think so. They were young couples—first time buyers. Don't think they even knew what they were really looking for or what they could afford." Again with the hair. What the fuck was she up to? My suspicion about the affair was growing by the minute and starting to eat away at my fragile state. Oh to be still in my dream, roaming free without a care in the world.

"Anyway, I need to get going, got a busy day ahead of me. Hopefully I can make a sale or two today. Good chance I'll be a little late tonight again."

I gulped heavily on my coffee as my anxiety magnified. Not a good idea—it was steaming hot, but I refrained from reacting. I didn't want to let on that I was agitated, or that I'd noticed her suspicious behavior.

5

Lying Cheating Whore

What would I do today? Wasn't in the mood for job seeking and daytime TV was a bunch of crap. Anyway, my mind was now racing. Was she really cheating? It was time to find out.

As I drove to the local bookstore, my plan was slowly coming together. I arrived, still questioning if I was doing the right thing.

The store was extremely quiet as I entered, with only a light scattering of college students swatting up on their studies. I felt uneasy as the closing door creaked behind me, disturbing the tundra like silence. The stereotypical librarian woman—strangely similar looking to my ex-colleague Pamela—peered menacingly at me over the glasses perched on the edge of her nose like a trainee tightrope walker, but managed to give me a forced smile as I headed to the lifestyle section. I found a book on the "Tell Tale Signs of a Cheating Partner" and began flicking through the pages. In a way I felt rather pathetic. Was this really required? Time would tell. I found the section "Five Tell Tale Signs of a Cheating Wife."

1   She's not as needy as before
2   She doesn't get angry anymore
3   She's being secretive
4   She places the focus on you
5   She showers you with pleasure

Jennifer had never really been the needy type anyway, but was certainly less in need than ever before. Anger didn't factor in anymore either. We were prone to our quarrels, like any other married couple, but this certainly had subsided in the last month or so, as we were essentially leading separate lives. I couldn't fathom whether she was being secretive or not—maybe to a degree. She wasn't as open as before, but perhaps that was just a result of her not caring too much, although she wasn't very forthcoming this morning on her whereabouts last night. She definitely deflected the focus onto me, which seemed like an attempt to get off any subject relating to her activities. Point number five though was a definite "no", so maybe there was still hope that she was remaining faithful. I scribbled down the five-point checklist and headed on my way. I wasn't paying $18.95 for that bunch of crap. Being the airhead that I am, I'd probably end up leaving it on the coffee table by accident, or anywhere around the house that she may stumble across, although I suppose that would be one sure way to find out if number two was actually true.

As I waited in the parking lot outside her Real Estate office like a private detective, my mind shifted into top gear. What was I really doing here? I felt like a stalker. What was getting into me? Why not just bring the subject up with her and have a proper adult discussion. Maybe I could be tactful with my approach, rather than steaming in with all guns blazing. "Jennifer, I've noticed we've been growing apart lately. Is there anything going on I should know about?" Yeah, that might work. Better than coming straight out with an infidelity allegation and making a complete jackass of myself if it wasn't the case. Just as I decided that was the way to go and head for home, she appeared from the office door with a tall, well-dressed gentleman. My plans took a complete u-turn.

I followed closely, but not close enough to cause suspicion. I watched enough detective movies to understand the drill. They had at least taken separate cars, so perhaps he was just a client looking for a house. They pulled up at a beautiful detached home on the posh side of town and I parked discretely behind a large SUV, not near enough to be conspicuous, but close enough to keep an eye on the house. He was a good looking guy, maybe early forties and very well presented in his suit and tie. He appeared as though he could afford a place in this neighborhood anyway. They proceeded in through the front door. There was no touching or glancing—it appeared to be all business, which set me at ease a little.

The minutes passed, but seemed like hours. She was certainly being thorough with the tour. I wanted to go up to the house for a closer look, maybe peer in the window or something to make sure all was above board. I talked myself out of that for two reasons. One, that was verging on being a complete nutcase and two, knowing my luck a neighbor would call the cops or something to report a peeping Tom—did not need that hassle. My life was screwed up enough right now.

Almost thirty minutes had passed and my anxiety level was off the charts. The house didn't look that big. Maybe she had clinched the deal and was finalizing some paperwork. That would be sweet. The commission on a place like this would be a nice chunk of change, and I could then tell her about the lay-off without us having to worry about money. Get everything out in the open and our marriage back on track. Between the commission money and my pity severance package, we could take that second honeymoon, start fresh and have enough left over to give me some time to find another job.

The front door opened and there they were. To my delight, all seemed in order. Then I noticed it. My heart felt like it had been plunged by a dagger. I can be a stickler for detail and a lesser man would have missed the subtle defect. His hair was definitely different. It had an almost ruffled look to it, not like the pristine condition it was in only half an hour ago. His tie was slightly undone as well. There was no doubt in my mind they had been fucking. That lying cheating whore, I couldn't stand it any longer. Shock, panic and anger simultaneously charged through me. My emotions were on an out of control ride—I had to get out of here. I wanted to jump out and confront them, but that seemed the easy way out. I wanted to hear it from her. If confronted, would she confess or continue being the lying cheating whore she had now become?

I paced the living room awaiting her return. My afternoon had been spent replaying the earlier events in my head over and over again. I was still in a state of shock. I had no idea how I would react when I saw her. The sick feeling in my stomach intensified every minute closer to her return.

My daze was suddenly halted by the sound of a key in the door. Holy shit, it was finally going to come to a head. Before she appeared in view, I quickly sat myself down, looking relaxed—well as relaxed as I could possibly be under the circumstances. I appeared almost hassle-free as I greeted her entrance.

"Hey Jennifer."

"Hey," she replied, almost seeming a little on edge. No fucking wonder—cheap little hooker.

"How was your day? Show any houses?"

"Fine, how was your day?"

Wonderful, what a real detailed and enthusiastic reply. Back to the five-point tell tale signs checklist. Number 4—'she places the focus on you'. Just answer the Goddamn question bitch.

"I had an interesting day—nothing special. You seem a little preoccupied Jennifer, can I assume you had no luck selling any homes today either?"

"Yeah, it was a slow one. Didn't even show any today never mind get a sale."

I immediately lost all sensation in my body. Fortunately I wasn't standing up, or I'd be sprawled out like a lifeless mess on the living room carpet. The term lying cheating whore would be branded on her forever. I was overwhelmed and had to escape. How could she look me directly in the eye and tell me that bare faced lie?

"Anyway, enough about my day," she muttered. More number 4.

"Fair enough."

"Let's get out of here Calum. Let me take you out for dinner, my treat."

What the hell was this? Number 5 was finally appearing—I had the full set now, not that it mattered anymore, the evidence was concrete and well past the "tell tale sign" phase. Her guilt must have been eating away at her for her to suggest going out for food, especially suggesting it as her treat. Yeah, great plan you little cow—how could that even balance the seesaw in her mind. Fuck some other dude, but buy me dinner and we're all straight. That angered me and I really had to get away.

"No can do, got plans for tonight, a work thing. We're taking one of our key customers out for a meal. Things aren't going too well with them, so need to butter them up a little. Anyway, I'm running a little late, so I need to get going—catch you later."

"You going dressed like that?"

She had a point, as I resembled a street vendor of a Homeless Newsletter. My appearance hadn't been top priority today, and to be honest I really didn't give a crap. Between having no job and a marriage headed for the scrap heap, being homeless might unfortunately fit into my future escapades, so this might be good practice.

"Yes I am, it's a casual affair," I said, half slamming the door behind me. Even the mention of the word affair had the veins popping out of my neck.

6

The California Roll

I got into the car and headed to the Tiger Bar, barely being able to concentrate on the road. My blood was boiling. I resisted the temptation to call Rachel—for now anyway. It was too early to get revenge in that way. Oblivious to the world I was brought back to earth with the sound of the siren behind me. The blue light was flashing, so I pulled over. I really didn't need this shit right now and wasn't in the mood for some arrogant cop to treat me like I was a teenage kid. What had I even done?

I watched in my mirror as he got out of the car. He had the typical "I'm so important" strut as he approached. I rolled down the window, anticipating his smugness.

"Is there a problem officer?"

"License and registration."

From his tone I could tell he was a real character!

"License and registration sir."

Why did cops have to have such attitudes? They were just everyday people. Why did so many jump on the power trip?

"I was only asking what I'd done."

"License and registration, then I'll let you know."

What a complete dick. I really didn't need this jerk-off right now. As I reached over to the glove box, he piped up again.

"Nice and slowly now, don't want to see any sudden movements from you."

Was this guy smoking crack? Did he think I was going to quickly pull a gun like Doc Hollywood or something? I couldn't believe this guy, so I handed the documents to him in super slow motion.

"That slow enough for you?"

"No need for the sarcasm, I'm just doing my job."

I watched again as he strutted his fat ass back to his vehicle. I had nothing to worry about—I'd never been in trouble with the law in my life. I knew he'd be disappointed when he ran my details and it came back clean. He had my address now, so I figured I would mess with him when he came back.

There he was again with the strut. Did they teach them at the police academy to walk like that?

"Did you realize you did not come to a complete halt at the stop sign back there?"

"I'm pretty sure I did."

"No sir you did *not*. You did what we call in the trade a California Roll."

California Roll? When did a sushi reference make its way into the traffic cop handbook?

"California Roll?"

"Yes, you almost came to a halt, but kept rolling forward, then proceeded."

This guy sounded like a robot with his monotone, yet he still managed to have a smug look about him.

"Shouldn't you be trying to catch real criminals?"

"Sir, you broke the law and I'm going to have to give you a ticket. I would also appreciate less of an attitude."

I had an attitude. Did he know what type of day I'd just experienced. Not that he would've given a crap.

"Whatever officer, just write me the ticket and I'll be on my way."

He scribbled on his pink piece of paper and handed it to me.

"Have a nice day," he said with a grin.

"I'm just glad you pulled me over now and not later. I'm probably going to be completely wasted when I get home."

I pulled away with a smile on *my* face. That would get him thinking.

I made my way into the Tiger Bar, giving the familiar doorman the nod. No request for identification as usual. They had a sign saying 'I.D required for under 40'. I was hoping the doorman was just using his common sense and that it wasn't a sign of my fading young looks. I really did have to start using that moisturizer to iron out some of these lines.

To my pleasant surprise, a familiar face was sat at the bar.

"David, what the hell you doing here, I thought the other night was a rare event?"

"Hey Calum, good to see you. I just had to get out the house for a while, the wife is driving me crazy. Nothing I do right now seems to be good enough."

"I hear you. Things on the home front aren't exactly going to plan for me either. Figured a few beers was what I needed tonight."

"What you having?"

"I'll take a Guinness as usual please David".

"You got it."

David had a very glazed look on his face. Seemed like he'd been here for a while.

"Had a few already?"

"Yeah, been here for a good hour or so. As soon as she got home from work tonight she started on me. Work's getting the better of me right now, so the last thing I feel like doing is home improvement when I get back at night. They are laying people off, but still expect the same amount to be done with fewer people. Amy doesn't seem to understand that I need some down time. It's not like her either, but it seems like constant nagging right now. I couldn't take it tonight, so here I am."

"I don't know, can't live with them, can't kill them," I said with a chuckle.

"You got it. Anyway, let's forget about them for now and get a few cold ones in us."

"Cheers," I said, clinking our glasses together.

"To happier times," said David.

We chatted for hours, keeping off the subject of our personal troubles. It wasn't an easy proposition though, as the occasional flashback jumped into my mind. I could almost visualize Jennifer working her way down the body of the guy in the suit. The more I drank, the more they entered my head. I didn't want to share the events from today with David as I didn't feel I knew him well enough for that. The last thing I needed was advice from a guy who was having problems of his own. I needed to talk to a woman, get some perspective on things from their side. Maybe I would call Rachel tomorrow—yes, that's what I'd do.

I had to get out of here, the visions of infidelity were getting the better of me, besides, I was pretty drunk and the last thing I needed was more beer. David decided to hang around for a while—he really could put back the alcohol. He'd already had a four beer head start on me and was craving for more. I arranged to meet him at the weekend for a few pints and headed on my way.

As the fresh air hit me, my head began to spin. The journey home was filled with my images of Jennifer and the mystery man. They were looking and laughing at me as they devoured each other's naked bodies.

Finally my house was in view, and to my delight, California roll cop was waiting outside the driveway, his arm hanging out the open window of his pig vehicle. My earlier comment must really have got to him.

I got out of the cab and looked over to his vehicle as I staggered towards my front door.

"Told you I'd be wasted. I'm sorry, did I forget to mention *I* wouldn't actually be the one driving?"

He looked furious, but I continued on into the house without looking back.

7

Die Suit and Tie Guy

I hovered above the crowded village again, my feathered friends treading air behind me, awaiting my next move. My super vision honed in on the busy main street. The same truck driver as before was surprisingly weaving his way along again. Another resident was distracted on his cell phone and heading towards the roadside. It was like deja vu all over again. I had to act swiftly to save the day. Without further hesitation, I made a nosedive to the applause of my troops. They loved it when the day was action packed.

As I neared the community, the man on the cell phone was becoming more familiar by the meter. I switched my vision to zoom. His image would be etched in my mind forever. I slowed down my speed but maintained the same course. My velocity may have altered, but the truck driver's had not. Would I make it there in time to save the day again—absolutely not, screw the suave looking prick, with his ruffled hair and undone tie. I activated my magnified hearing. It was just as I thought.

"I can't wait to see you as well" he said in his pathetic lust filled tone.

"As long as you give me as much attention with your tongue as the last time," said Jennifer in her frisky sounding way.

Not much chance of that honey. Die suit and tie guy—you're going to get what's coming to you.

The screech of the truck's brakes caused suit boy to realize his upcoming fate. He dropped the cell phone and matched the truck with the intensity of his scream. He was sent like a Tiger Woods drive down the village road and almost as far. I was only a moment too late—what a pity!

The village was in a panic as people ran frantically around in sheer despair and shock. The only survivor was the cell phone. I picked it up and noticed it was still connected.

"Patrick, Patrick," came the shriek from the receiver.

"Patrick's going to be otherwise engaged for a while. Looks like you'll need to find another tongue to service your needs you lying cheating whore," I said with a chuckle before closing the flip.

I sat at the edge of the road with my head buried in my hands. My performance was Oscar like as I faked my sadness. I was quickly surrounded by a group of the local people.

"Don't beat yourself up Calum, we know you did your best. You can't always be everywhere at the right time," said a caring elderly lady as she put her arm around me for comfort.

"I know, but it doesn't make it any easier for me. If only I'd been a few seconds sooner."

If only they knew. It had been a good day, almost as satisfying as saving a young girl's life.

I awoke with a sudden jolt. The dream remained crystal clear in my mind. I felt wonderful, just like the last time. It was like a stress relieving session. My plan had been to get psychological counseling to help with my current problems, but these dreams were almost like medication in themselves. They were a hell of a lot cheaper as well, and under my current jobless situation, a more viable option. The expense part was not necessarily true though, as this recurring dream had only ever happened after I'd been under the influence of alcohol. I had no idea of the reason behind this, but I wasn't about to mess with it right now and was already looking forward to my next session at the bar. Maybe I'd try a different pub next time.

I had the house to myself as Jennifer had already left for the day, probably working, but more likely working on suit boy's penis. The idea of this didn't bother me as much, which was weird, as I still felt satisfaction from his unfortunate road accident. That did not make sense either as I knew it was fiction, but at the end of the day I was feeling better about things and that was all that mattered.

I sat with a cup of coffee and two slices of heavily buttered toast and made a call to my old office. I was put through to my previous department, and to my delight, Rachel's familiar and sexy voice answered.

"Hey good looking."

"Calum, how are you?" she said gleefully.

"Well done, I didn't even need to identify myself."

"I'd recognize your voice anywhere. Didn't expect to hear from you so soon."

"Yeah, I know, but I wanted to say hi and also ask you a favor."

"Sure, whatever you need."

"You available for lunch or has Carter got you snowed under due to his incompetence as usual?"

"No I'm free today. He's gone to head office to take part in the whole business restructuring thing due to all the lay-offs."

"Restructuring eh, more like how can they get together and justify further head count reductions."

"Probably, but I hope not. I really don't need that potential hassle right now. Anyway, what were you thinking for lunch?"

"Well, there's this English bar on the high street that apparently does great lunches. I've never been, but David said the food is great and very reasonably priced as well."

"Sounds great, what time should I meet you?"

"Well, that's where the favor comes in. I was out for a few beers last night and decided to get a cab home, so my car's still in town. Would you be able to pick me up?"

"Of course. Now I see why you want to go for lunch with me."

I knew she was kidding around, but I felt I had to justify myself.

"Not at all. I was thinking about you and figured this could kill two birds with one stone."

"I'm just teasing Calum, I'd be more than happy to pick you up."

"Great stuff, see you around 12:00pm?"

"Sounds like a plan. See you then."

I felt a sense of self-accomplishment after the call ended. Rachel was a great girl and a looker as well. Maybe I would act on her advances if she made them again. More likely she wouldn't though. All her inhibitions had gone the other night, likely due to the huge alcohol consumption. Even if that was the case, I was still thinking about it. I had two hours before she was due to arrive, so decided to finish up my coffee and toast and then jerk off. It was purely a precautionary measure. It had been so long since I'd been with a woman in that way and would likely ejaculated at the slightest mention of the word sex, never mind the act itself, so better to empty the tank now and perhaps I'd at least last a decent length of time if the situation came to fruition.

I cleaned myself up with one of the dirty socks lying at the end of the bed and headed for the shower. My imagination had been running wild, and it had been as satisfying a hand session as I'd had in ages. I'd contemplated putting on some porn, but was so eager to start the proceedings I figured my mind could capture the same effect. Jennifer had entered my head, but a quick flashback of her and her mystery man put that to rest. Rachel would be the star of my fantasy and we were back to the night at the Tiger bar. She was groping me under the table, but this time it was only the two of us in the bar. She pulled down my pants and handled me like a true master. We kissed passionately as we played with each other. It was just beginning to get really interesting when I could hold my release no longer. I laughed out loud as I climaxed. It was a good decision to jerk off. If the real situation had arisen without it, there was no way I would've even lasted as long as the pitiful two minutes that'd just gone by.

I dried myself off pretty good and even shaved my pubes. Be prepared was the motto of the day, and upon inspection my penis looked a little bigger with its new trimmed look. I was feeling great and looked forward to lunch with Rachel.

8

The King's Head

The journey into town was an interesting one. Rachel was on good form and genuinely pleased to see me. She chatted non-stop and I paid attention as much as possible. My mind was regularly wandering back to my masturbation session only an hour ago. She was dressed in a little business type suit, although instead of pants, she had the matching short skirt. It was driving me crazy and was the cornerstone for the flashbacks to my one handed fun. Maybe something of a physical nature would happen with us today, but I would play it cool for now, although it was obvious she was interested. Her body language was extremely flirtatious and she had definitely put on some make-up and a fresh application of lipstick prior to her arrival at my place.

We entered the King's Head bar, it was packed, but a good sign the food was of a decent standard. It was filled with business suit types, not unlike Jennifer and her new lover. Tables were few and far between, but we found a cozy little number in the corner, which was perfect, and secluded enough for Rachel to grope me under the table without being detected. I really had to simmer down a little, but in reality that wasn't going to happen, as it was all I could think about.

"What you going to have?" said Rachel, seemingly looking for suggestions.

"Not sure, a lot of items are a little unfamiliar to me, but I'll probably go for something typically English though, thinking about the Steak and Ale Pie."

"I'm going to go for the fish and chips."

"That sounds good, maybe I'll join you on that."

The waitress arrived and I ordered the food and a couple of soft drinks for us both. I could see Rachel gazing at me as the waitress jotted down the details. Think she liked the fact I was taking charge.

"Do you know what day it is today Calum?"

"Wednesday as far as I'm aware," I said in my most sarcastic tone.

"Very funny, do you know what occasion it is today?"

"Nothing is springing to mind, but with all that's going on in my life right now, I'm not surprised if I've forgotten something."

"It's my birthday."

"Shit, I'm sorry Rachel, I had no idea. Maybe we can go and buy you a present after lunch or something."

"Don't worry about it, there's no reason you should have known. Buy me a couple of glasses of Pinot Grigio and I'll forgive you."

"You've got yourself a deal."

The idea of a few drinks was music to my ears. I'd been choking for a beer, but didn't want to give Rachel the impression I had a problem or something. However, as she'd initiated things, it was fair game now.

The food was delicious—much to my surprise. It made a nice change to the typical lunchtime chicken fingers or cheeseburger. The beer was going down well and the wine had brought a little glow to Rachel's cheeks. Her flirting increased with every sip, as did my eagerness to be with her.

"We should probably get going. Don't want to keep you late getting back to the office."

"I suppose," she said with a sigh.

"Maybe we can do this again sometime."

"I'd like that."

As we walked back to her car, the wind was gusting past us, and the aroma of her sexy perfume was like a constant stream. It was delicious and really beginning to turn me on.

"So where did you leave your car?"

"The Tiger Bar parking lot." I was so caught up in the moment that I'd almost forgotten about that.

The short ride to my vehicle was a little awkward. We were both very quiet, which was a complete change. I was a little nervous as I knew the end of the date was approaching and wasn't sure if I should just get out of the car and say goodbye, or whether I should give her a kiss on the cheek. Perhaps she had something of that nature on her mind that was contributing to the silence.

"Well here we are," she said, pulling into the vacant spot beside my car.

"Yep, here we are."

My heart was starting to pound. I had to make a quick decision about how I was going to end our lunch date. There was an uncomfortable pause, before Rachel broke the silence with what can only be described as music to my ears.

"So do I get a birthday kiss or what?"

I was definitely taken aback, and stuttered and stammered a little before moving in towards her eager lips. It was exhilarating, and exceeded any former expectation, and totally different from the way Jennifer kissed. Rachel's lips were fuller and there was a delivery of passion that had been missing for longer than I can remember. Her tongue was like an electric eel working its way through an underwater cavern and her fingers weaved through my hair at a frantic rate. This amused me as I had another flashback to Jennifer and suit boy with his ruffled hair coming out of the empty house after their horizontal get together. If Jennifer happened to be watching right now, she would see how it had felt for me. Well it was my turn now, and I was going to make the most of the opportunity.

"I should really let you get back to the office," I said, reluctantly pulling away.

"I've got a better idea. Why don't I take the afternoon off? Carter is out of the office and it's not likely he'll be in touch. They're likely having their meeting offsite, involving posh meals and large quantities of alcohol at the company's expense. The last thing on his mind with a few drinks in him will be calling to talk to anyone here."

"Sounds good to me, what did you want to do for the afternoon?"

"Calum, you're a smart guy, I think you can work that one out for yourself," said Rachel with her sexy little wink.

I was super horny now, and although surprised by the turn of events, was eager to get this show on the road. I wasn't a religious man, but for some reason I looked quickly to the sky, thankful that I'd decided to jerk off earlier. What an asshole I was. Like God had sent me a signal, encouraging me to spank the monkey on the off chance I committed adultery!

"I was hoping you'd say that. I'll meet you at the Bay Hotel in five minutes."

I was trying to play it cool as I quickly left her car, giving a swift look back and returning the wink.

We sped like it was the deciding race in the Nascar championship, jockeying for position, tires screeching as we made the final turn before the hotel. The place was nothing flash, which was fine. It wasn't like we were planning a long weekend there, with fine dining and a few suave late night shows. It was fit for its purpose though—cheap, clean and not unfamiliar to a long list of Mr and Mrs Smiths on their guest book during midweek afternoons.

We closed the room door behind us and the frenzy began. It was like a scene from a movie as we virtually ripped each other's clothes off. I threw her onto the squeaky mattress and started to work my tongue over every inch of flesh on her body.

9

Jennifer

Where had it all gone wrong? It was hard to locate the specific root cause, but routine had played a large part. Calum was a good man, in fact he was more than that. He was smart, funny and definitely good looking. He would never be a male model, but he was a real manly man, with his chiseled features, five o'clock shadow and inclination for watching football on a Sunday afternoon.

We first met at college. My first impression of him was that he was a smart ass, which he was. He was friends with my girlfriend Tina's boyfriend. They would always go out after class on a Friday afternoon for a few beers and meet up with us girls later in the evening. They were usually a bit drunk by that point and any inhibitions that may have existed were long gone by then. Calum was very opinionated and appeared to disagree with any political viewpoint I would have. As it later turned out, he told me he would just do it to get me a little aggravated—he said I looked sexy when I was irritated. He once asked me if I'd ever kissed a guy with a goatee. When I responded that I had not, he asked me if I would like to. It was a little cheesy, but cute at the same time. I still thought he was a bit of an ass though.

My opinion of him changed one evening at the college library. It was a foul night as the rain was pouring down. It had came on suddenly and I wasn't exactly dressed for it. We met as he was leaving the building. I was standing at the exit door, hoping the rain would subside.

"Hey Jennifer, how's it going?"

"I've been better."

It was obvious I wasn't in the most talkative of moods. It had been a long and boring day of lectures and the last thing I needed was to be stuck here on campus any longer. To my pleasant surprise, he removed his raincoat and without giving me a chance to object, he placed it over my shoulders.

"Looks like you need this more than I do," he said with a very pleasant smile. I was so used to him being a bit obnoxious, but then again, I don't think

30

I'd ever been with him socially while he was sober. Perhaps deep down he was-n't such an ass after all. The gesture was certainly a welcome one, and his smile was very comforting and adorable at the same time.

"You're going to get soaked," I said almost concerned.

"As long as you don't, I'll be happy. Let me grab those books for you."

We walked and talked, as we headed in the direction of my apartment. The wind howled and the rain seemed to pick up in intensity. That didn't seem to phase Calum at all, as he remained perky and maintained his sweet smile, often cracking jokes about how wet he was. He said if there was ever a good time to pee himself, it was now, as nobody would ever know. There was a certain charm about him that hadn't been exposed to me before—I liked it.

We eventually arrived at my apartment building and made our way up the steps to the entrance door.

"So this is where all the fun parties happen."

"I wouldn't quite go that far. They're more Jessica's doing than mine."

Jessica was my roommate, a trendy, good looking blonde girl, who was very popular around campus. Our place at weekends was like a continuous social gathering. A group of us would hang out and get a little buzzed before heading out to the pubs. Money was tight and we all struggled to afford an evening of bar priced drinks.

"Whatever you say, I'm sure it's *you* that's the innocent one," he said with a smug little grin.

He was standing there like a drowned rat as I handed back his raincoat.

"Come in and get dried off, it's the least I can do."

"Thought you would never ask."

He was definitely a smart ass, but in a different way than before. As we made our way up the stairs, my mind flashed back to earlier in the day. It was a chick thing, but we took pride in having a tidy home. All was good though. I was organized by nature, and although the place was often littered with empty beer bottles and take out cartons at the weekends, they never stayed there for long. As much as a party girl that Jessica was, she could be as particular as Monica from Friends at times.

"Take off your clothes and go take a hot shower."

"Take it easy Jennifer. I don't usually go that far on a first date."

"You know what I mean wise guy. I'll stick them in the drier for a while and you'll be good to go."

"That's a shame, thought it was my lucky night."

"Whatever you say Casanova. Who said this was a first date anyway?"

"I'm just messing with you. I know it's not a first date *yet*."

"Just get in the shower you crazy boy. There are plenty of fresh towels on the top shelf."

The drier was on and I sat on the sofa watching Fear Factor. It was the grossest show on TV, but entertaining nevertheless. This boy was definitely growing on me. What was he doing in that shower? Hopefully not what I was thinking, but then again it was like an addiction to all the guy friends I had.

The door opened and out he came. I nearly fell off the couch at the site. He had a bath towel wrapped around his naked body like a cocktail dress and had another around his head turban style—like most women were prone to doing.

"Does it suit me?"

"You have some serious issues," I said trying to suppress my laughter, but it was a hopeless task. He sat across from me on the lazy boy chair.

"Don't worry, I'm already seeking professional help."

"Close your legs or something. I don't need a view of your meat and two veg."

"That's the second date, right?"

The irony of it all was that he was correct. He left that evening with his dry clothes on and we exchanged a peck on the cheek as he said goodbye. I agreed to meet him for a drink the following evening. We got a little intoxicated and ended up fucking like rabbits until the early hours of the morning. We were together ever since and the sex only got better. We were so compatible and both opened minded enough to try anything once. The chemistry was indescribable.

Even after we were married, our sex life only flourished. To end up in the pothole we landed in was nothing less than tragic. Why had I cheated on him? I know I needed the attention, not to mention a real penis. I was going through batteries like the Duracell factory for a while, but I'd had enough. It was no excuse. I should've had it out with him, sorted out our issues like an adult. No point in having regrets now though. I'd committed adultery and needed to deal with it. The sex with Jonathan was nothing to write home about, but he made me feel special and filled a void in my life that had vanished long before. It was time to put an end to the affair. At the end of the day, I still loved Calum.

10

Horny Hypocrite

The guilt overtook all of my feelings on the way home from my afternoon rendezvous. I was such a fucking hypocrite. I was the first to judge Jennifer for her infidelity, but I was no better. It was about revenge before, but the feeling had changed now that I'd accomplished my own dirty deed. It had changed things forever and there was no way of taking it back.

The entire experience with Rachel wasn't exactly how I'd pictured it. Don't get me wrong, she was a wonderful kisser, but her bedroom skills weren't a patch on Jennifer. She just lay there like a sack of potatoes. There was no changing of positions, and the earlier passion in her car had dried up like a prune. They say the grass is always greener on the other side. One thing was for sure, the grass was certainly bushier on the other side. Rachel's bodily grooming left a lot to be desired. Her pubic region was like a mini version of Sherwood Forest. As I was going down on her, I was half expecting Robin Hood to pop out and shoot me with an arrow. My earlier worry about not lasting very long was never in jeopardy. In fact, my real worry during the proceedings was that I would lose my erection. She was doing nothing for me and I was just going through the motions. I had to close my eyes and pretend I was making love to Jennifer in order to keep myself hard—it was pathetic. As I climaxed, I let out a satisfied groan, more in delight that it was all over than actually being satisfied with the experience. I rolled over onto my back, and to my dismay, Rachel snuggled into my side like a lovesick puppy.

"That was fantastic Calum," she said cuddling even tighter.

"Yeah, pretty good." Not the most sincere of replies, but it was all I could bring myself to commit to.

"I could just lie here forever."

Those words echoed like the screams from my worst childhood nightmare. I needed to get out of here. What could I possibly say? One thing was for sure, I couldn't tell the truth.

"Yeah, me too, but I'm going to have to get out of here soon. I'm meeting my Lawyer this afternoon to discuss my divorce options."

"That's OK. Do you at least have time to have some wild sex again before you go"?

Of course I did, but I couldn't. Wild was the last adjective in the world I would've used to describe what had just happened, but I ran with it.

"Unfortunately I don't. I need to go home and make myself look a little more presentable before heading back into town. Maybe we can do this again sometime?" The lies were just rolling off my tongue.

"I'd like that," she said, again tightening her grip on me again. She was getting very clingy. I don't know why I expected anything different. Women were way more emotionally involved after sex. Guys could just treat it for what it was. She didn't seem too disappointed I was leaving though. Perhaps it was because I'd mentioned divorce. Maybe she was hoping I was going to push it through as quickly as possible and then we could be together. That was never going to happen. She was a sweet girl, but the chemistry wasn't there and I couldn't get Jennifer out my head now—I was still in love with her. I put my clothes back on in record time, boxer shorts and socks inside out, but there was no time for delays.

"Where's the fire?" said Rachel, struggling with her bra strap.

"I just don't want to be late. Want to create a good impression." Again with the lies, but at least it sounded convincing.

I handed the key back to the reception desk and checked out. The girl behind the desk was obviously onto us. We had only checked in an hour before.

"Have a good day Mr. Smith," shouted the receptionist as we left.

I turned around and she gave me a rye little smile.

The drive home was an emotional rollercoaster. Why did I feel so bad? Getting even had seemed like a great idea at the time. Now it felt like the biggest mistake of my life. Not only had I cheated on my one true love, but I'd led on another girl, which only added another set of complications to my already fucked up life. I wanted to run away, keep driving as far as possible and come back in a month or so, with everything the way it was when I'd first got married. I was beginning to scare myself. What was happening to me? Maybe I'd get drunk and fall asleep. Get back to my happy place of flying around and saving the day. People needed me there. They respected me and there were none of the daily pressures that existed in this screwed up world. Drinking wasn't the answer right now though. It was time to be a man and face up to the consequences. I had to sit down with Jennifer and talk things through once and for all. Regardless of the outcome, it was time to sort out my life, one way or another.

11

Be a Man

I sat miserable on the sofa, praying Jennifer would come home soon. The more time that passed, the more chance I would be a coward and not have the discussion I should've had with her a long time before now. I thought that things were beginning to get clearer in my head, but I couldn't have been more incorrect. The fact I was still in love with Jennifer had only added another variable to an already complex equation, and I was no mathematician. Perhaps it was too late for it all. Just then, there was the familiar sound of her key in the door. There was no going back now. It was finally time to be a man.

"Hey," I said. Not the opening I'd planned, but at least it was a start.

"Hey," she said with an inquisitive look on her face. She knew there was something on my mind.

"We really need to talk." She looked uneasy, probably thinking I might be onto her infidelity. Little did she know I had been for a while, but that was unimportant right now, especially after my conduct earlier this afternoon.

"This sounds serious."

"It's very serious, and extremely important to me right now. Sit down, this might take a while."

"Can I get changed first, I've been in these clothes all day?"

"Just sit down, I need to get this off my chest right now. It's been bottled up inside me for months. If I don't get it out now, I might never get the courage up again and I'll probably regret that for the rest of my life."

I hadn't meant my tone to be as severe, but I was desperate. She sat down very tentatively. She knew we had to talk at some point, but was obviously nervous about what was about to come out of my mouth. I was virtually shaking. I'd rehearsed a little earlier, but my mind was a blank right now.

"Life together recently has been hell to say the least. I can't go on like this for much longer as it's slowly driving me insane."

"There's the understatement of the year."

"Please let me finish Jennifer. You've no idea how difficult this is for me, so please let me get this off my chest and then you can say whatever you like!"

She was taken aback by this, but adhered to my request. She could obviously tell I meant business.

"I know I contributed greatly to pushing us apart, with my long hours at work, high stress levels, lack of affection towards you, as well as a reduced sex drive. I should've been more of a man before this and communicated openly with you, rather than being a stubborn prick and ignoring it, hoping things would return to normal on their own. I was wrong and a real asshole to say the least. However, communication is a two way street, and the fact we're so alike, especially when it comes to stubbornness, hasn't helped the situation in any way or form."

I paused and took a deep breath. The next part was as tricky as it could possibly get, but I was on a roll and had to keep going.

"I don't want to go into a lot of detail about this or how I know, but I'm aware you've been doing certain things recently that seriously compromise our marriage vows. Don't try and deny anything or tell me any further lies." She almost seemed to be in shock by this, but her blushing told the whole story.

"I haven't exactly been on my best behavior in that department either. I am ashamed of myself, but can't keep it locked up in my mind any longer. I feel like my head is about to explode with all the secrecy and lies in our lives right now. I've been telling myself it's over for so long now. But the closer I get to the realization of it all, the more I recognize that I still love you Jennifer—I always have and always will. Now you can have your say."

I sank into my chair. My speech had taken no more than a minute, but I felt mentally exhausted, but physically refreshed at the same time. There was a moment of silence. She was staring intently at me as her bottom lip began to shake. The quivering accelerated at an alarming rate and was suddenly replaced with uncontrollable sobbing. Her tears flowed like an open faucet onto the coffee table. She tried to say something, but her words could've been Chinese, as her violent bawling made every one of them virtually incomprehensible. I felt strangely bad for her—wasn't sure why, but got up and put an arm around her nevertheless. This only intensified the tears. She was human after all, but had been like an ice maiden for months now. This was back to resembling the Jennifer of old—a woman with passion and feelings.

"Come on now sweetheart, it's OK."

She looked at me with her bloodshot eyes.

"I do still love you as well."

It was like music to my ears and she could tell. My smile caused her another tearful convulsion. It was good to see such feeling, but I wished she would stop.

I was struggling to keep my emotions together and was about to accompany her with the weeping chant.

"Why didn't we get this out in the open before Jennifer?"

She calmed a little and dried her eyes with the sleeve of her blouse.

"I don't know Calum. We're both too stubborn for our own good."

"No shit Sherlock. I don't want to lose you honey—that much I do know. Do you want to give this another try?"

"More than you could ever know. I need to think things through though, and want to do this properly this time. I think we should spend the night apart and establish how we're going to deal with any problems going forward, how we're going to keep the fire burning, stuff like that."

"Sounds fair enough."

"I'll spend the night at my Mother's and I'll come over tomorrow morning and we can talk more."

"Fine by me, I know there's a lot to sort out, but I know we can make it happen. There's one thing I do need to insist on though. Anything of a physical nature that's happened with anyone else is off limits. I don't need to hear any details and I'm sure you don't either—deal?"

"Deal," she said with embarrassment. She didn't look too happy with me though, but couldn't criticize. I was going to keep my betrayal to myself, but a fresh start would best begin with honesty.

We shared a loving hug and a soft peck on the cheek, before she went through to the bedroom to get changed. I felt like celebrating. Maybe I should've mentioned about losing my job, but I didn't see that being a big issue, it would all form part of a fresh beginning. She hated my job there anyway. It had contributed to the demise of our relationship, so I was convinced she would almost be pleased.

She appeared in the living room about fifteen minutes later with her overnight bag.

"I'll call you tomorrow," smiling as she said it.

"Can't wait."

We shared a warm embrace before she headed out to her car.

"I do love you Calum."

"I love you to Jennifer. See you in the morning."

As her car left the street I let out a joyous scream, falling back onto the sofa and kicking my legs in the air like Tom Cruise in the movie Risky Business. It was time for a celebration, nothing fancy, just a few cold beverages—I think I deserved a couple.

I didn't want the inconvenience of driving or catching a cab into town, so I decided to go along to the Raven Tavern. It was a local bar at the end of Raven

Road. It was a nice night, so I decided to walk—it was only about fifteen min-utes away and I could avoid the hassle of driving home with a few drinks in me. Would just be my luck to have California Roll cop waiting to bust me. The day was going well now and I wasn't about to mess with that.

12

Raven Road Bridge

It was like walking on air. I felt stress free for the first time in months. The walk was a pleasant one and time sailed past quicker than ever. The bar was at the other side of the Raven Road Bridge, hence the name of the establishment. It was decent enough as far as bars go. I hadn't been in a while, but it would serve its purpose. It was a bit of a sawdust on the floor joint, but from what I remember, it was friendly enough and served a killer pint of Guinness.

As I crossed the bridge, the view was a thing of beauty. It was a clear night and you could see for miles out over the valley.

The Raven Tavern was just how I remembered it—a little run down, but cozy all the same. It had never been that crowded in the past, and the drinks were dirt cheap. There probably wasn't much left over cash for any fancy renovations. There were only three guys sitting at the bar, none of who even raised an eyelid as I sat down. It was still early, so hopefully the place would pick up a bit later.

I wasn't one for regularly frequenting bars on my own, but recently with all that was going on in my life, as well as the discovery of my drunken wonder dream, it had been on the increase. Each of the three gentlemen were scattered around the bar, and appeared to be on their own also. Two were exchanging some chatter from their respective positions, but from the sound of the general banter they were having, it was just to alleviate the boredom. It made me wonder if they were all going through some personal problems like I had been. That was history now. I was in the best of moods and ready to socialize. My sweetheart was back in my life again and it was time to celebrate. In the next few days we would hopefully be together and I could feel the passion again that had been missing in my life for so long.

"Can I get you something to drink?"

The bartender was an attractive woman in her early forties, with what can only be described as mammoth breasts. It almost looked like Tele Savalis and Yule Brunner's heads were stashed in her low cut top, obviously fake, but would make some good viewing if things became a little dull.

"Hi there, a pint of your finest Guinness please and whatever these three gentlemen are having."

"That's very nice of you," she said with a pleasant smile.

"It's been a good day. Get one for yourself as well."

"I really shouldn't, working and all that."

"I won't tell if you won't," I said with my trusty wink.

"Well maybe just a little one."

"That's the spirit."

I watched intently as she poured the Guinness. It fascinated me the way it settled. It was like watching the sand steadily flow from an hourglass. She even finished it by etching a traditional Irish Shamrock into the creamy foam head, which was a skill in itself.

"Very impressive."

"Lots of practice. I've messed up so many times, but I think I've got it down now."

"I'm Calum by the way."

"Nice to meet you Calum, I'm Jennifer. But please call me Jen," she said as we exchanged a handshake.

"Nice to meet you Jen. Funny, my wife's name is Jennifer."

"You're married. That's a shame."

She gave me a cute little wink and walked away. If I was a single man I would've been all over her like a rash, but I wasn't about to screw up my return to happiness.

"These are on Calum," said Jen as she placed the fresh beers on the bar for the three lonely gentlemen.

"Thanks," they said in unison.

"You're very welcome guys, any of you up for a game of darts?"

They all agreed rather quickly. There wasn't much else going on, so the simultaneous positive response wasn't surprising. They were all in their late forties to early fifties, and as I discovered, they'd obviously shot darts on more than one occasion.

"So what brings a young guy like yourself to this little shit hole of a bar? Figured you would be out in town living it up," said the elder of the three guys.

"Not tonight, just wanted somewhere low key that served some good cheap beer."

"Well you certainly came to the right place. It should pick up in a little bit though, tonight is Karaoke night. Do you sing?"

"Only in the shower, unless I've had a gut full of beer of course."

They all chuckled at that. Obviously touched a nerve.

"Well, we'd better get you working on that beer then. Jen, another pint for Calum when you get a chance sweetheart."

"Coming right up Frank."

Frank was a bit of a character, which was a complete contrast to my initial impression. The other two, Jim and Bob were decent enough, but no match for Frank's razor sharp wit. He had a kind looking face, but there was a twinkle in his eye that suggested he was a bit of a ladies man back in the day.

After giving me a sound thrashing on the dartboard, we congregated back at the bar. These guys were obviously seasoned drinkers, but I was determined to match them beer for beer. Couldn't let a bunch of older gents show me up. Besides, I'd had a lot of practice recently and was starting to build up quite a tolerance.

A steady flow of people began filing into the bar. Upon each arrival, Frank gave me a brief rundown on their Karaoke skills. None of his descriptions were particularly flattering, but very amusing all the same.

"If you've ever wondered what it sounds like to strangle a cat, stick around and listen to Peggy."

Peggy was in her mid to late fifties and dressed for a night out at an upscale restaurant. She obviously took the singing seriously and thought she was a bit of a performer. I would definitely have to see this.

It was a diverse crowd. A good mixture of couples and single folks and a fair spread of ages—although I still figured I was likely the youngest. This was probably why Jen the bartender was giving me a regular glance. No doubt it was refreshing for an older chick to get some attention from a younger guy.

The singing was well underway, each one worse than the next, but entertaining nevertheless. Karaoke without shitty singers was like Russian roulette without the bullets. My head was beginning to spin a little and my vision was becoming blurred. Jen's humungous breasts had become four, which made me smirk to myself. I'd barely be able to handle the two.

"Next up we have Calum," came the cry from the microphone. I looked around to see Frank laughing. That old prick, I knew he was a prankster. I reluctantly stood up, egged on by the cheers of the crowd. I only knew one song—Blue Suede Shoes by Elvis. I knew there was word assistance, but it helps the flow if you already know most of them.

I belted it out the best I could, putting on my best Elvis impersonation. The crowd was a blur and my inhibitions were gone. I finished off with the trademark "Thank you very much." There was rapturous applause and I staggered my way back to my seat.

"Good job young man, thought you only sang in the shower."

"Cheers Frank. Nice trick by the way, I'm going to start calling you Frank the Wank."

"Wank," he said with a confused look.

"Yeah, it's a British term for jerk off."

"Frank the Wank—I like it. You're OK kid, a lot more fun than most of these sour faced old farts. Hope you come back here again, I've enjoyed your company."

"Oh, I'll be back Frank, you can take that to the bank."

I ordered us another beer, just in time for Peggy to take center stage. Another drink was the last thing I needed, but I wanted another close-up of Jen's tits before I got out of here.

"I'll take my check after this one sweetheart."

"Leaving me so soon, that's a pity. Come back and see me sometime."

"I'll be back," I said, putting on maybe the worst Arnold Schwarzenegger impression in the history of mankind. It was certainly cheesy, but Jen got a rise out of it.

Just as Frank had stated, the cat choking commenced. She looked like mutton dressed as lamb, quite a combination with her rendition of Whitney Houston's "I will always love you." It was obvious she thought she was something special as well. If I were to make a guess I would've said she was tone deaf. I was worried for all the beer glasses in the place—shattering being a definite possibility. She reminded me of some of the contestants from American Idol, the ones on the early audition shows. Those who go in with such conviction and compare themselves to a present day superstar, only to be told from Simon that they're as talented as one of his balls, and then be all surprised by it, telling him he must be crazy.

Enough was enough, I had to get out of here. It had been a fun evening. I said my goodbyes to Frank and the boys and blew Jen a kiss as I left. Not to my surprise she returned the gesture.

The fresh air hit me like a Ferrari. What was it about that that made you even more wasted? I'm sure there was some scientific explanation, but in my current state I didn't really give a crap. I headed towards the Raven Road Bridge on my short journey back home. It was going to be a longer trip home due to my constant staggering, but that was OK, I had the knowledge of being reunited with my sweetheart again, so all was good.

The view out over the valley was as wonderful as ever, even though my vision was hazy to say the least. The Raven Road Bridge had been a landmark for many years and served as the major link between the town and rural communities. It was breathtaking—so peaceful and untainted. I could've spent the night there, but was extremely inebriated and getting awfully sleepy. It was time to take my ass home.

13

The Bungee Boys

The view was spectacular—I loved the Raven Road Bridge, and so did my feathered buddies. We would regularly hang out there, hoping the bungee boys would show up. They were a great bunch of guys and so much fun. They loved their bungee jumping, but were a little jealous that I didn't need a chord attached to me.

To our delight, the boys were there, hooking up their equipment, ready for a night of jumping.

"Hey Calum, great to see you, are you going to join us for a few jumps this evening?"

"I wouldn't miss it for the world."

"We like it when you're here. Makes us feel even safer knowing that if anything goes wrong with the bungee chord, you'll be there to save us."

It was nice to be appreciated, but these guys weren't afraid of injuring themselves, if anything they thrived on the intensity of it all. They were all extreme sports enthusiasts. BMX biking, snow board jumping and sky diving, just to mention a few. If there was an element of danger involved, these guys were interested.

We perched on top of the safety railing of the bridge, eagerly watching them set-up their equipment. We loved joining them in a swallow dive, as they plummeted towards the bottom of the valley. They would fall two at a time, screaming and hollering obscenities as they fell. They were a real crazy bunch, but knew how to enjoy themselves and make the most of life. I was blessed to have the gift of flight. I would always ensure I reached the bottom before they did. It was great fun for me also, but at the end of the day I was a protector and made sure there were no unfortunate accidents. My feathered friends began to chirp with excitement. They had seen this many times and knew the boys were almost ready for the first set of jumps. Finally they were hooked up and ready to go, standing perfectly balanced on top of the safety rail.

"You ready Calum?"

"Ready as I'll ever be."

"OK, on three. ONE, TWO THREE."

The rush was incredible. Their screams of excitement were almost deafening. I loved hanging out with the Bungee Boys.

14

A Mere Mortal

Where was Calum? Surely he hadn't had second thoughts about giving our relationship another try. He seemed overjoyed when we spoke last night. Perhaps he was now regretting the whole agreement. His bed wasn't made, but then again, not many of the male species make that a daily habit, so it wasn't a good indicator of being home or not.

Why was I being so negative? He knew I had my key, so perhaps he'd popped out to buy some breakfast stuff for us. He'd always been great at that during our early days. He was so cute the way he pretended to be a master chef. He would toss the eggs in the air and break them on the edge of the spatula as they fell, before beating them like an uncooperative war prisoner. To his credit, he made a wonderful omelet—bacon and cheese being his specialty. Mmmm, bacon, eggs, cheese, maybe a couple of sausages and some heavily buttered toast. My mouth was watering at the prospect, and for the first time in longer than I can remember, I was really looking forward to him coming home. This time would be different, and I was determined to make it work. We needed to communicate more, pick up on any early signs that we were getting into a rut, and take actions there and then to spice it up again, not ignore it like before, and just hope it got better on its own—that didn't work, which was one of the only good things we'd picked up from our marriage. At least we had learned and could do it differently this time. Most couples in similar circumstances just ventured down the quick road to divorce as their first port of call. What'd happened to marriage these days? It had long departed from the sacred bond it had once been.

I put on a fresh pot of coffee. I was like a little schoolgirl anticipating her first kiss as I danced merrily around the kitchen. I poured myself a cup, sat down in front of the TV and put on the local news, just as the telephone rang.

"Ladies and Gentlemen, this is the early morning local news. A young man's body was discovered earlier this morning at the bottom of the Raven Road Bridge. It's unclear how this occurred, but evidence shows he must have fallen in some way from the bridge top and would have died instantly. Police are still investigating the scene and currently calling for any witnesses. It is unclear whether this was a suicide attempt or if any foul play was involved. At this time, the man's identity cannot be revealed as the police are still attempting to contact his family."

The Crap Shoot

The Crap Shoot

1

Running from the Knees Down

Last night had been a blast—Bachelor parties always were. The group consisted of mainly married guys, whose social lives had diminished considerably since their "big day". As a result, we tended to really let loose when the chance came around. Last night was no exception. It was beer and strippers galore, but the after hours Indian meal was definitely a mistake, and taking its toll on my stomach right now.

I ran from the knees down towards the public restroom, but wasn't sure I could contain it until then. I chuckled, thinking that the Indian food probably looked better on the way out. Laughing in my current state was a huge error, as I almost lost control of my ass muscles. Fortunately they reacted like a coiled Cobra, and saved a rather embarrassing mess, not to mention an equally uncomfortable trip home on the Subway.

The restroom was located in the public park, situated close to the entrance area. It was a ghastly looking little building, often frequented by dubious individuals to say the least. I usually avoided public lavatories like the plague, but emergency situations require drastic measures. I darted through the entrance, almost knocking over an elderly homeless guy who probably lived there. The place was foul, and I mean rancid, and smelled like a shit had just taken a huge dump. I had no time for the customary bowl inspection. It was normal public bathroom procedure, whether at the office, a bar, or even this festering joint, to work your way down each stall until finding one sanitary enough for you to bare your butt to, followed by stacking the seat approximately four feet high with toilet paper, but ensuring you left enough to clean your ass with afterwards. However, that luxury wasn't even an option. I burst through the first door, whipped down my pants in mid-stride and landed on the nasty seat, not a moment too soon. The Chicken Tikka Masala exited like a bull from the rodeo gates. The relief was indescribable, and easily outweighed the situation of being perched on one of the nastiest toilets in the country. I was in a cold sweat. Every time I thought the ordeal was over, another echoing rumble invaded my stomach.

Finally the agony ended, and my head sank with relief into my open hands.

"No fucking way," I said rather loudly, but it just came out by instinct. I thought the situation couldn't get any worse, but to my horror I was miles from the truth. The agony of seeing an empty toilet roll holder pained me like I'd just sat on my balls. It almost brought a tear to my eyes. There was no way I was just going to pull up my pants and pretend it never happened, I'd have a swarm of flies chasing me the entire way home.

Just as I was preparing to waddle my way to the next stall, I heard the voices of a father and young son entering the bathroom. The place had been silent—other than my trumpeting ass—the entire time, but now some dick and his mini dick son decide to arrive at the most inopportune moment.

"Daddy it stinks in here."

"It's a public toilet Brian, they all stink."

He was absolutely correct, it was rank when I first arrived, but I was sure I'd hiked up the stinkometer a notch or two since then.

"Not that one Brian, there's no toilet paper."

No fucking way, there were only four cubicles in the place, and now I knew at least two were paperless.

"Yuk, someone's jammed the roll down this one Daddy," screeched little dick Brian.

Oh my God, three down, one to go.

"This one has paper son, a little anyway, although there might not be much left after I clean this seat. Take your time kid, I'll be right out here when you're finished, just shout if you need me."

I wanted to shout for some toilet paper, but couldn't bring myself to do it. What was the big deal in asking for some paper? Women would do it without any problem, or so my wife had once told me. Being a man was different though, especially in a public park restroom where everyone was a stranger. The unwritten rule was to say nothing or as little as possible. I prayed that young Brian wasn't much of an eater and would only pass a couple of little nuggets, requiring no more than a sheet or two.

"Brian, you OK in there?"

"Yes Daddy. The paper's finished."

"Is your butt clean?"

"Yes Daddy."

That little prick, probably one of those kids not trained by their parents to look at the paper after each wipe. I knew of people who didn't. How the fuck do you know when you are clean? You can't just say, "I always use eight sheets."

For one, that could be detrimental to the environment if five would have suf-
ficed, and secondly, the number of sheets required is directly proportional to
the consistency of your shit. There should be a mathematical equation developed, that is communicated from Kindergarten onwards. I was sure that little
cock could've saved a sheet or two.

My liquid mess was a definite ten to twelve wiper. Even if there had been five
or six pieces left, I could have attempted the delicate procedure of wipe, fold
and wipe again. It was usually a little messier and required the touch of a surgeon, but was bearable as long as you thoroughly washed your hands and
underneath your fingernails afterwards. Knowing my luck, there would've
been no fucking soap either—not that it mattered now. I had to figure out
what I was going to do.

To my alarm, more voices entered the bathroom. It was apparent they
must've been shady looking, as "Daddy" ushered Brian outside at lightening
speed.

"Come on Brian, let's go. You can wash your hands when we get home."

Whoever came in really must have looked like trouble. Telling your young
kid to leave the crap on his fingers until they got home was strange to say the
least.

"Keep watch dude, and don't let anyone in here until we do this," said one of
the new voices.

Keep watch? Don't let anyone in! Until they do what? My heartbeat
increased dramatically. What a day this had been so far, and it wasn't even midday yet.

"This is some good coke dude," said voice one.

I think it was a fair assumption he wasn't referencing the soft drink.

"Dude, there's someone in that toilet, I can see their fucking feet," said voice
two in a real thuggish tone.

Crap, I had to think fast.

"Hey, who the fuck's in their dude?" said thug one, banging on the door.

Everything was "dude" with these guys. I felt like I was in a scene from Bill
and Ted's Excellent Adventure. Perhaps there was a deleted scene somewhere,
where a "dude" with diarrhea dripping from his crack, embarrassingly gets his
ass beaten by the two wasters. In my best stereotypical retard sounding voice, I
replied.

"I'm going poopy. Do you like going poopy?"

"It's OK dude, it's just some fucking retarded dude," said dude one to dude
two.

If anyone sounded retarded, it was these guys. They were incapable of delivering a sentence without using their favorite word at least twice.

After some fine chopping and snorting sounds later, Bill and Ted headed on their bogus journey. I was alone again and had some decisions to make. Perhaps I could take the cardboard roll, tear it into smaller pieces and try using that. It probably wasn't very absorbent though—would likely just spread the shit around as opposed to wiping any up, so that was out. Maybe I could jam my butt into the bowl as far as possible and flush it a few times, might have a similar affect to a French bidet. This place was a festering haven though. Who knew what dangerous bacteria were living in that bowl—the thought turned my stomach. I'd rather be pursued to the Subway station by that swarm of flies, than leave here with a clean bottom only to wake up in the morning with an asshole infection. There was only one solution, I had to sacrifice my Calvin Klein underwear. Jockey-shorts in hand, I started to wipe.

Oh come on, not more fucking people, not now. Their voices were deliberately whispering, but were close enough for me to interpret.

"Twenty for a hand job and thirty for a blow job."

The seller sounded a fairly young guy, but the buyer appeared to be older. I think I got a brief glance at some grey hair through the very fine seam of the doorway.

"Let's go with the blow job, I can't give myself one of those."

What kind of place was this? Firstly, class A drug taking, now there was gay prostitution. What was next, bestiality?

It sounded like they went into the end cubicle. I was surprised they hadn't noticed I was in here or at least checked for the presence of somebody, before going headstrong—so to speak—with their illegal rendezvous. I had to get out of here. I restarted swabbing my ass crack with my CK's. The wiping rate accelerated with every cock slurping sound coming from my new rent boy neighbor. It was almost making me gag.

Finally I wiped and looked at the underwear. Sweet, that one didn't leave a mark. However, my bright white Calvin's were now looking back at me like someone had been throwing chocolate at them. I tossed them on the floor like the piece of garbage they'd now become, and bolted out of the place like a cheetah. Like little dick Brian, I wasn't hanging around to wash my hands either.

I continued running until I got to the duck pond. The park itself was a very quiet and peaceful place during the day, but I hadn't been at night before. There were several nature walkways as they were called. People loved to run, jog and walk their dogs, especially in the morning. It was a real friendly place, except for the bathroom as I'd discovered.

In my case, I just liked the park for the tranquil environment. Its serene nature enabled me to think clearly and be at my creative best. I loved people watching also, it was a lot of fun, so many different looking folks, unusual mannerisms and other little intricacies that fascinated me. I was a writer—a struggling one to say the least—so anything that could contribute to the development of a character was generally jotted straight into my notebook. Today was not one of those days. I'd come to the park for a walk, in the attempt to clear this hangover. I had to get out of my apartment, the more I lounged around there, the worse my headache became. I just wish a couple of my buddies had come along, I could've used the support back at the nasty assed restroom. My head was almost clear, and although I'd left the notebook at home, threw around a few ideas for a story. I needed to publish something of substance, money was tight, and the immediate future didn't look much fucking brighter. My wife Debbie was a nurse at the city hospital, and even her measly salary trounced the pitiful income from my pathetic column in the local newspaper. It was time to write a novel with some zest to it, or at least a large multi-episode article for a national newspaper or magazine. Maybe my disastrous experience from today could be used to create something appealing? I gave it some thought as I headed towards the edge of the pond and finally washed my hands.

2

Write or Wrong

On the short Subway ride home, I thought long and hard about the story potential of today's incident, until a lady in her eighties sat down beside me and commenced some pointless, not to mention annoying conversation.

"Isn't the Subway great, beats the dreadful bus service that's for sure. Those buses are so unreliable. At least you can count on the Subway," she said in her little old lady voice. She sounded like she had been a smoker for about fifty years, and her blue rinse tightly curled perm only enhanced the amusement of it all.

In a way I was happy she had sat down next to me. I was a little paranoid that in my panic to leave the bathroom, maybe I'd missed a few dollops of shit. In my experience, old people generally smelled like a mold and piss cocktail anyway, so if someone got a whiff of crap from my location, they'd likely think it was Granny Smith here.

"Yes, I love the Subway as well," I said, just for the sake of it.

"The bus service used to be reliable back in the day, but not any more young man. Too many people now, cluttering up the place, especially all those illegal immigrants. None of them can afford cars, so they take the bus and there aren't enough buses to go around, it's leading to all sorts of problems."

This was riveting stuff! I was beginning to lose the will to breathe. Thankfully it was my stop.

"Nice to meet you," I said, as I quickly made a dash out of the door like it was a public lavatory.

I felt bad for the next poor bastard who sat beside Granny Smith. I could just picture her telling the same story over and over again.

I entered our apartment as quiet as a mouse, with only the occasional creaky floorboard potentially giving my presence away. Debbie was working nights right now and usually slept until the early afternoon. She was a heavy sleeper, so it was unlikely she would've heard me. I could hear her though, she could've made the Olympic snoring team and probably contend for the gold medal. I would often make fun of her for it, but even to this day she didn't believe me. I always told her I would tape her one night to prove my point, but I never followed through with it. She was such a cute little thing and I didn't have the heart to bring it to her attention for real. Women were so sensitive about these things and I didn't want her to be all self-conscious.

I rustled up a quick fried breakfast, sat at the kitchen table with the local paper and reviewed my latest article—it sucked. It was a piece I'd come up with, exposing the sordid nature of phone dating lines. It had seemed like a good story at the time, but they never seemed to read as well after I read them in published print.

Debbie and I had met at the local chat line. We weren't regular callers, but actually worked for the dating line company during our time at college, in order to make some extra money. To the other callers, we were just one of them. After connecting to the line, each person provided their "name" and a brief message. From here they could enter the chat line. Then they listened to ads from those on the line, and if interested, they could use their touch-tone phone to request a live chat, send a recorded message or skip that person and move on to the next. That was how we just slipped into the crowd. We would create our fictional profiles and participate just like the others—without incurring the overpriced phone charges of course.

Our sole purpose was to engage people in conversation, be who and what they wanted to be, and keep them on the line for as long as humanly possible. At ninety-nine cents per minute, this could equate to a nice little chunk of change. It was a commission based job and actually made us more money than we were now. Chat lines were big business, with frequently hundreds of people on the line at any one time, some believing it was another avenue to find their soul mate, others were just lonely looking for someone to talk to and pass the aching hours. The majority however, made the line what it really was, a sordid, sexually charged place where people could indulge anonymously in their secret fantasies.

That was the premise of my newspaper article—exposing these lines for what they really were. Many people called looking for love, but mostly it was filled with perverts looking for a cheap screw or prostitutes avoiding the added dangers of hanging around street corners.

"Afternoon sweetheart, did you have a nice time with the boys last night?"

Debbie had surfaced, her powerful snoring nostrils had probably picked up on the scent of my bacon and eggs.

"Hey gorgeous, nice to see you. Yeah, last night was a blast, was suffering this morning though."

We exchanged a kiss and she headed to the refrigerator for some orange juice.

"Well, I've no sympathy for you. You're out gallivanting and I'm giving bed baths to crusty old men."

"Stop it, you're turning me on! Those old guys were probably as sexy as some of the strippers at the club last night. I gave them a few dollars, but mostly out of sympathy."

"Right, sympathy, of course it was."

What I said wasn't exactly true, but there were a few of the girls who just didn't cut it as exotic dancers. At one point we were actually concerned for the pole, and had a few bets going as to how long it would take for one of the ladies on the Big Mac diet to bring it crashing to the stage.

"There were a few nasty looking ones though and none of them were a patch on you sweetheart."

"Danny, stop talking shit. Learn to quit while you're ahead."

"OK, I'll stop now, but you *are* gorgeous."

I really did mean that. I'd fallen in love the moment I set eyes on her. She was beautiful, a real head turner. Her shoulder length dark hair was magnificent, and always had a scent to it that caused me to melt. Her skin was blemish free, with an almost Latin style look about it—I loved her more than life itself. The weird and wonderful thing about our first encounter was that it looked as though she'd just rolled out of bed at the time, with her ruffled hair, black sweat pants and white t-shirt which was obviously an old favorite, as it was a little frayed around the edge of the collar and sleeves. She was still stunning and I could only imagine what she would've looked like with a lick of make-up and a cocktail dress. It took her a while to warm to me, but eventually it happened after many hours of persistence from my side, the rest was history. With us being called Debbie and Danny, we were known back then as the "Double D's", a reference that'd continued with our friends to the present day.

"How did your article turn out?"

"OK I think, but they never seem to read as well as I first think they do. I really need to do something to improve our lives, this local newspaper gig just isn't going to cut it going forward. I need to start working on something that's going to bring us in some serious money. I'm going to give my writing one last shot honey. If it doesn't work out, I think it might be time for a career change."

"I've got faith in you Danny."

I loved her even more for that. She supported me with every endeavor. I felt I was letting her down, but I had a plan.

"Let me run this idea past you and let me know what you think."

3

The Plan

Debbie listened intently, as I detailed the plan for my latest project. It was based on my earlier experience at the park, and she almost wet her knickers laughing as I described almost shitting my pants, then having to wipe my ass with my underwear.

"I bought you those Calvin Klein jockey's. Fifteen bucks they were. Maybe I'll buy you a brown pair next time, just in case."

"Very funny honey, you wouldn't have found it so funny if it'd been you."

"Oh come on Danny, you have to admit, it's hilarious. I'm sure it wasn't that funny at the time, but it's over now."

"I'm kidding, I know it's more than a little amusing. Honestly though Deb, I almost had a fucking heart attack when I discovered there was no toilet paper.

"My poor baby, maybe if you go wash your ass I'll make you feel better, a lot better, if you know what I mean."

You have no idea how tempting that was, but I wanted to finish explaining my idea, and perhaps put a detailed plan together. I was as excited as I'd been in a long time and only hoped Debbie agreed.

"I was thinking that I could hangout at the public restroom in the park on a regular basis, and do a complete story of the goings on there. From what I saw today, there's a lot to write about. I was thinking about a balance between the idiosyncrasies of people's public restroom habits, and the sordid activities such as drug use and gay sex going on, basically in our backyards. It could be a nice combination of comedy and hard hitting facts. If what I experienced this morning is anything to go by, just imagine what that place is like at night."

"It certainly sounds like an interesting idea Danny. My only worry is that it sounds a little dangerous. I mean, you don't know what sort of criminals could be hanging out there in the evening, I'd be a little worried about your safety."

"I understand sweetheart, but I'm excited about the potential of it all. I've thought about the potential dangers and decided that going undercover is the way to go."

"Undercover? Are you going to turn into an FBI agent or something?"

"Very funny, you're certainly on good form today, that's for sure. No, I was thinking more of disguising myself as a homeless guy. There seems to be a bit of homeless activity there as well at times, think they use it as a place to crash. I would fit right in and wouldn't arise any suspicion. Drug dealers and prostitutes are not going to feel threatened by some waster lying about drunk in the corner."

"Still sounds dangerous to me, but I'll support you with whatever you decide to do."

"I hoped you'd say that darling. Now what was that you were saying earlier about making me feel better?"

4

Salvation Army

I worked my way meticulously through the racks of clothing. They were all pretty gross and not exactly the height of fashion, so I really wasn't sure why I was being so fussy. The Salvation Army place was way busier than I expected it to be. Were people really that interested in finding a bargain? I assumed that the clothing would've been washed before going on display, but from the smell of the place, I was beginning to doubt my assumption. Why did I care about that though? The whole plan was to find a few items that looked and smelled like crap.

I decided on a pair of slightly stained, brown colored jeans, with several worn patches on them. Even at three dollars, I didn't feel like it was a bargain. I grabbed another few items, equally revolting, but would look perfect for my homeless character. The finishing touch was a baseball cap. I wanted to be as disguised as possible, and the more I could cover my face the better. The last thing I needed was for somebody to recognize me at the park. Knowing my luck it would happen at the most inopportune moment and blow my cover and the entire story with it.

No more shaving for a while either—Debbie was going to love that! She hated kissing me when I was all jaggy. Well it wasn't the actual kissing part that bothered her, more the graze marks that were left on her face afterwards. I think it was the fact it was visible to her colleagues at work, and they'd tease her senseless about it. She never complained to me about the stubble burn if it was located on her inner thighs though!

"Is that all for you today sir?" said the cheerful cashier.

"Yes thank you."

"Would you like to contribute a donation towards our disaster relief program?"

Money was really tight at the moment, but I couldn't bring myself to decline. As much as I complained about my life, I suddenly realized it wasn't that bad. At least I had a home, my health, and a beautiful wife who loved me dearly.

"Sure, just add another five dollars to the total."

"Thank you sir, that's very kind of you," she said, as her already beaming smile became even brighter.

I really should've been thanking her, as the majority of these people were either volunteer workers or paid a pittance, and helping those less fortunate than myself.

I grabbed my stuff and headed for home, feeling a little guilty and thinking about how lucky I really was.

I contemplated washing my high fashion garments before putting them on, but appearing homeless and smelling like fabric softener was a definite contradiction. It grossed me out as I pulled on the crusty brown pants. Who knew where they'd been. The non-matching navy blue sweatshirt was equally as disgusting, but it clashed beautifully with the pants, making it almost perfect for the task ahead. The baseball cap and dirty old boots added the finishing touches, and I made my way to the living room to strut catwalk style for Debbie.

"Rrrrrr, hold me back you sexy beast," she said, laughing almost uncontrollably.

"So do I look homeless?"

"Danny, homeless people will probably be handing *you* some spare change."

I adored her sense of humor, it was so refreshing, unlike my appearance.

"Excellent, I was hoping you'd say something like that, as long as I look convincing."

Tomorrow morning would be my first day on the job. The plan was to sit in the corner of the restroom and observe the various people who frequented the place. I'd even made up a little cardboard sign saying "Spair change pleez, hoamless and hungray". A homeless person's sign was never as effective if the spelling was perfect.

I'd arranged to meet a few of the boys tonight for a couple of drinks. It was probably going to be my last night out for a while, as I intended to pour my heart and soul into this project. It also gave me the opportunity to tell the boys of my plan and perhaps get some useful inputs from their side. Another consolation of a night out would be looking and feeling like crap in the morning, which would only compliment my desired appearance.

I met the boys at our favorite bar in town, a trendy little Irish place by the name of Connor's Shamrock. The owner was actually called Connor, but he was as Irish as I was African American. I think he had been to Ireland once, but that was about the extent of it. We were regulars to the place and Connor would often greet us with phrases like "Top of the morning to you". For one his fake accent left a lot to be desired, and secondly, it was generally in the evening when we frequented the place, making his gesture a little redundant. He was a good guy though and often gave us a round of drinks on the house, which was always appreciated.

"So what's this project you're going to be working on then?" asked Jeff as he sparked up a Marlboro Light.

Jeff was probably my best friend. I'd known him for many years and he had an incredible appetite for alcohol, and would often be drunk four or five evenings of the week. The only reason his wife put up with him was because her craving for dirty Martini's was on par with his beer consumption.

"I'm going undercover as a homeless person for a book or newspaper article I'm going to work on. I haven't decided which one though."

They all stared at me rather blankly.

"Going undercover as a homeless guy?" responded Jeff quizzically.

I went into detail of my adventure at the public restroom, much to their delight. My intentions now seemed to be a little clearer to them.

"Better be careful Danny, who knows what kind of fucked up people will be hanging around there at night. Don't worry though, anyone gives you any shit and I'll knock the pricks into next week," said Graeme in a reassuring fashion.

Graeme was the tough guy of our crowd. A really placid guy by nature, but you didn't want to get on his bad side. He was about six feet five, ruggedly handsome, and built like a sprinter. In his spare time—as well as drinking pints—he trained in mixed martial arts, the stuff they do in the Ultimate Fighting Championship, so his words of reassurance were more than just that.

"I don't know Graeme, maybe he's just looking for some young dude to blow him for thirty dollars. Is this your way of coming out of the closet Danny?"

Jeff was such a wise ass, but we were always bursting one another's balls.

"Yeah Jeff, you've got me figured out. Just don't drink too much tonight and lose control, you don't want me popping my cock into your mouth when you're passed out."

Andrew and Stuart found this particularly amusing. They were twin brothers, both very fond of the opposite sex. They were good looking guys, who had the advantage of not requiring the use of chat-up lines when they were at bars. They would just stand at the bar together and women would ask them "are you guys twins?" The very nature of the question was extremely unnecessary, as Stevie Wonder could've told you they were twins without having to ask. However, all you need is a woman to initiate the conversation and you up your chances considerably, as far as scoring for the night. The women who typically asked this were not usually academically gifted, but this suited Andrew and Stuart. They weren't looking for a relationship, just one that lasted until breakfast. They shared an apartment together. One night Stuart went home with a beautiful blonde who had the IQ of a deckchair. In the morning after a night of horizontal pleasure at their apartment, Stuart got up and told Andrew how good she'd performed. Miss USA was still sleeping, and for a joke, Andrew got undressed and climbed into bed with her. She ended up banging him, and to this day, is still unaware that it wasn't Stuart.

We drank until the early hours before heading home.
"Call me tomorrow night and let me know how your first day goes."
"Will do Jeff, take it easy guys."
"Yeah, remember Danny, any shit goes down and I'm only a phone call away."
"Thanks Graeme, much appreciated big guy."
It was very heartening to know I had such good friends.

5

First Day on the Job

As expected, I felt like shit. My head was pounding and my mouth was as dry as the bottom of a birdcage. I reluctantly dragged my ass out of bed and headed towards the bathroom like a zombie. The cold water on my face was just what the doctor ordered, but I resisted every temptation to jump in the shower. My outfit for the day was disgusting, so why shouldn't my body be the same.

I wolfed down a couple of slices of toast and a large glass of juice, before climbing into my tramp outfit. It didn't look any better on me today. In fact it looked even worse as a result of my bloodshot eyes and scruffy facial hair. I grabbed my cardboard sign, mini-tape recorder, enough change for the Subway journeys, a few dollars for a bite to eat, and headed on my way.

I was certainly getting more attention than usual. People were staring, and one woman and her young daughter appeared to cross the street rather than walk past me. It was no accident either. I turned around a few seconds after they'd switched sides, only to see them crossing back to where they'd originally been.

The Subway journey was equally as fascinating. For once I had loads of space. On occasions, somebody would look like taking the adjacent seat, but after setting eyes on me they elected to move further down the carriage. This was most interesting to me, and as I looked around I would catch people staring, only to immediately turn away as I made eye contact.

My heart started to pound as I closed in on the entrance to the park. I questioned why I was doing this, but was determined to press on. The bathroom appeared to be quiet as there was nobody hanging around. To my delight it seemed completely vacant as I entered the foul and revolting door. I checked each of the stalls, and rather ironically, three out of the four actually *had* toilet paper. Not for long though, as I removed each of the partially remaining rolls and disposed of them in the trash. It was mainly part of my plan, but partially as revenge. It would make for a far more interesting day if a few people shared my recent experience. I slouched myself in the corner with my sign on display, and waited for somebody to arrive.

Several people came in and out, but nobody of any significance, and to my disappointment they all went number one. It was mainly a couple of joggers and a few people out for a morning stroll. I was amazed though, that almost every one of them farted just as they started to urinate. I was always one for just letting it go, wherever and whenever, but there was such feeling of relief in their grunts and groans that it made me wonder if some people held it in until they found a bathroom.

Although it had been a little disappointing so far, I'd managed to accrue about a dollar twenty-five from the generosity of my farting friends. Just as I started to doze off, the sound of a few nearby voices caused my head to jolt completely upright.

"What are you looking at you homeless prick?"

The vicious nature of the comment really had me on my toes. There were two guys in their early twenties and a well dressed guy in his mid-thirties standing no more than a few feet from me."

"Leave the guy alone Gibby, he's just minding his own business."

I resisted the temptation to respond, and just dropped my head back down, as if I was going back to sleep. That couldn't have been further from the truth, I was ready like a mongoose incase I had to spring to my defense, but more importantly I secretly reached for my tape recorder.

Fortunately they went about their business, undeterred by my presence. It was a weird scenario. The gentleman in the suit had a briefcase with him and looked like your stereotypical lawyer type. The other two younger guys were obviously crooks of some variety.

"It's two fifty for an eight ball," said Gibby in his bullying manner. I was no expert on drugs, but I knew he was referencing Cocaine and not a pool table accessory.

The lawyer type counted out the money and went silently on his way. Gibby and friend were ecstatic with the score.

"You should go and get a real fucking job instead of hanging about in public parks," said Gibby, obviously directed at me, but I remained silent.

A real job! That was a laugh coming from the drug dealer himself.

"Leave the guy alone Gibby, he's not doing us any harm."

The other guy didn't seem so bad. It sounded as though he at least had a conscience.

"Fair enough Dano. Wait for me outside, I need to take a quick dump."

Retribution was all mine, you little drug dealing asshole. I wasn't a religious person, but life seemed to have a way of balancing itself out. There was going to be nothing quick about this dump, as long as he didn't notice the lack of paper, which from initial indications of his intellect, was highly unlikely.

The splash of the first drop of shit into the bowl was like music to my ears. It took me all my time to hold in the laughter. A few squeezes later were briefly followed by silence.

"MOTHER FUCKERS," he screamed, obviously kicking the door with his pants around his ankles.

Dano came busting back in.

"What's up Gibby?"

"There's no fucking paper in here. Get me some from one of the other toilets."

I watched and listened intently as Dano worked his way down each cubicle.

"None of them have any Gibby."

"FUCK. What kind of place doesn't have any fucking toilet paper?"

"What do you want me to do?"

"Go to the ladies next door and get some from there, those bitches are bound to have some."

For once he'd made some sense, I hadn't thought of that. Perhaps I would get here earlier tomorrow and remove those as well.

"What if there's some women in there?"

"Dano, I couldn't give a fuck if Laura Bush is in there cleaning her snatch, get in there and bring me back some fucking paper so I can wipe my ass before the shit starts to harden".

Off Dano went like the lap dog he was. He came scuttling back a minute or so later with enough paper to start a small bonfire.

Gibby cleaned himself up, much his relief. As he came out of the bathroom, I could see the sweat on his forehead. I was rather pleased with myself.

"Let's get the fuck out of here," said Gibby.

They went on their way without even saving goodbye. I let out my suppressed laughter and decided to take a break from the hilarity, and headed down to the duck pond. I would come back again just before dark fall and see what went on here in the evenings.

6

Well Blow Me

Sitting around the duck pond was more invigorating than usual. The cool fresh air breeze easily conquered the stench from Gibby's number two. After a short while, I headed to Jeannie's Café, a little place not far from the park. It was a cozy, family owned business with great food, but the customer service was never wonderful. That was another of my pet hates—lousy customer service. A decade ago, or perhaps a little longer, service in the States was far superior than it was today. The reasons behind this baffled me, as customer expectations hadn't changed. The service this afternoon was particularly bad. Maybe the waitress, Elizabeth, was having an off day, but it was more likely my appearance was the major factor.

"Cheeseburger and fries, with a large diet coke please."

She looked at me like I'd just asked her to fondle my nuts.

"I do have money you know," I said putting a ten dollar bill on the table.

"Oh, I'm sorry, I didn't mean to suggest that, I'm just having a bad day."

She scurried off in the direction of the kitchen, hopefully feeling like a complete asshole.

As I waited, I played back my tape recording from earlier. To my surprise, I'd managed to successfully press the record button while it was still in my pocket, and even more unbelievably, the sound quality wasn't too shabby. The drug exchange was legible, as was Gibby's agonizing toilet paper adventure.

I scoffed the last of my cheeseburger and settled up the bill, leaving a pitiful tip, and headed back towards the park. It was reaching sundown and I was eager to see what the evening had in store.

A new angle to my story developed as I neared the restroom. Standing outside the ladies end of the bathroom was an attractive looking woman with big hair, knee length boots, fur coat, and caked in make-up. She was a little rough around the edges, but definitely worth a roll in the sack after a few pints of beer. It didn't take Albert Einstein to realize she was a hooker. She gave me the once over as I walked past, but no proposition was made, which I wasn't surprised by. I was sure she didn't want to put any penis in her mouth that was attached to someone in my state, irrespective of the money offered.

I'd planned to resume my position inside the gents room, but in light of her presence, I sat myself down outside the entrance and again put my sign on display. It wasn't long before a potential client showed up, a semi-respectable looking guy in his early forties. I discretely switched on my recorder. He appeared a little nervous as he shakily walked past, obviously determined not to initiate anything, probably incase the lady of the night was just waiting on a friend, and not a prostitute after all.

"Looking for a good time?"

The words were obviously a delight to the gentleman, as he turned and approached her. He'd noticed me sitting around, but was not affected by my presence.

"What did you have in mind?"

"Anything you want, for the right price."

He was wearing a wedding band, so obviously things on the home front weren't living up to expectation.

"How much for a blow job?"

"Fifty bucks."

"What about anal?"

"That's going to cost you. One hundred usually, but I don't have any lube, so it'll be one twenty."

It certainly wasn't the Bunny Ranch around here. That would usually set someone back around a thousand, from what I'd heard. If the guy was really looking for a bargain, he could've waited around and had his last request satisfied on my side of the bathroom for half the price!

"I'll go with the blow job then."

She led him into the ladies room to fulfill his desperate needs.

They reappeared no more than a few minutes later. He seemed a little more concerned with me being there, probably because I knew he'd blown a load in Guinness Book time, rather than any illegal implication of his actions.

After he departed, the big haired hooker approached me.

"Looks like your night is even slower than mine," she said, dropping a few dollars in my lap.

"Thanks," I replied, in a genuinely surprised tone.

As she headed back to her side of the restroom building, I wondered how she'd got herself into this line of work. From her gesture she was obviously a thoughtful person. Had she been abused as a kid? Was she just broke, and had a child to support? Or did she just enjoy sucking cocks? I wanted to ask, but wasn't comfortable doing so, we'd just met after all. Perhaps if I ran into her on another evening, I'd strike up some sort of conversation.

The night was beginning to drag. The hooker had long since gone, maybe back to her family, or off to a more profitable location. I was just about to call it a night when I heard some male voices coming from the other side of the building, and they were gradually getting closer. Without a further thought, I swiftly made my way into the corner location of the male bathroom.

"I know it's a bit gross in here, but it's much safer than in the actual park, I've never seen the cops around here."

I pretended to be asleep this time, and they paid no attention to me.

"I've never done this before," said the other fellow.

"I promise I'll be gentle," he said, with an extremely girly laugh. "Your wife has no idea you're bisexual?"

"Not a clue. She's never been one for giving blow jobs anyway, so I figure this kills two birds with one stone."

"Well this little bird promises not to kill your two stones," he said, again with the lady like laughter.

It was actually quite a funny remark to come up with on the spot, but I couldn't laugh too much as I knew what activities were about to take place. The recorder was still running, so I put my hands over my ears. I couldn't handle another rendition of dick slurping. My first experience of such a musical was more than I ever wanted to deal with again.

I waited for a while after the sword swallowing was over before heading for home, as I didn't want to arouse any suspicion. My two visits to this place had been extremely eventful, drug taking and dealing, female and male prostitution, cheating husbands, closet bisexuals, not to mention embarrassing toilet performances. It had been a real eye opener and I was eager to get back the following day.

7

The Jerry Mitchell Band

It was great to see Debbie. I'd only been away for twelve hours, but it felt like an eternity. She'd been worried about me all day, and was equally glad to see me.

"I need to get going to work soon honey."

I hated when she worked nights, we never got much time together.

"Take the night off sweetheart and we can soak in a nice big bubble bath together."

"I'd love to Danny, but Bridget was off sick last night and unlikely she'll make it tonight either, so I can't let the other girls down."

"You're loss then, I'll just have to have some fun on my own in the bathtub," I said, half joking, but now that I'd mentioned it, I'd probably have a little spank of the monkey.

Relaxing in the tub was like I'd gone to heaven. I contemplated not bathing, but that wasn't an option, not after lying around in that filth all day. The bubbles were like silk and I could almost feel the grime peeling off my body. I'd left the door open, so the sounds from my stereo reached the bathtub with perfect resolution. I'd put on my favorite CD, the Jerry Mitchell band. He was a local artist, well renowned in the State, and had even made it on the national scene back in the day. It was such relaxing music, with some fabulous guitar rifts. There was no doubting his artistic ability, but I thought he was a complete dick as a person. I'd never forget meeting him when I was fifteen years old. It was right after his concert at the local arena, and I'd been lucky enough to win a radio contest, with the first prize of going backstage after the gig and meeting Jerry and the band. The concert rocked, but the entire time I was anxiously awaiting the moment I would finally meet my idol. I eventually got backstage to the band, autograph pen in hand and a copy of their latest album. I walked over to Jerry with a huge smile and reached out with the pen and album cover.

"Look kid, I've just finished a gig, can you wait a fucking minute and give me some space for fuck sake!"

It felt like my heart had been ripped out. For years afterwards I wouldn't play his records. How could he do such a thing? It was fans like me who made him famous, the ones who bought his records and paid to see his concerts. I was back playing his music now though. As much as he was a prick, his music was still great.

I jerked off in time to the beat, visually running my tongue up the length of Debbie's smooth and soft legs, circling her naval and then onto her breasts as the water splashed in time to the drums. Daydreams were weird, as I reached her neck it wasn't her head attached, it was the prostitute lady from earlier, with her big hair and make-up.

"That'll cost you twenty," she said.

I jumped to attention with fright, as bath water spilled on the floor. Enough was enough. It was time for an early night, as I'd had more than enough excitement for one day.

8

The Night Shift

The buzz from the alarm clock pounded in my head like a bad migraine. Four presses of the snooze button later, I decided to crawl wearily out of bed. I stumbled through to the kitchen on autopilot, and was pleasantly surprised to see Debbie at the table reading the newspaper.

"Hey honey, when did you get home?"

"About half an hour ago. You looked so peaceful, and I didn't want to wake you."

"How was your shift?"

"Crazy as usual. Bridget was out sick again, so it was non-stop running around, I'm pretty worn out."

"You'll be pleased to hear that I took a bath last night."

"I figured as much, the smell of shit's gone away."

"Very funny honey, it wasn't that bad."

"Danny, it was maybe even worse. I couldn't get out of the house quick enough last night. I still love you though, even though you smell like crap sometimes. Maybe if you keep this tramp thing going for a while I might get used to it. More likely I'll divorce you though."

"It'll be me divorcing you, any more of your wise ass comments."

"You love it and you know it. What time are you heading down to shit town today?"

"Not sure. I was going to go down in a little bit, but I was thinking that maybe I'd do a night shift instead. It might be more interesting as it is Friday, and I'd also get to spend some of the day with you."

"That sounds nice. Just as long as you don't think you'll be getting some loving."

"The thought never crossed my mind," I said, with my familiar eyebrow twitch and naughty smirk.

"I need to get some sleep. Alright for you, snoring your ass off all night while I'm out saving lives."

She didn't want me to get on the subject of snoring. When she worked nights, it was often the only time I got a good sleep. When she was home it often sounded like someone was trying to start a tractor in our bedroom.

"OK honey, your loss. My tongue was planning on running a marathon down town as well."

That certainly got her attention, as she paused on her way to the bedroom. "Well, what are you waiting for cowboy?" She didn't even turn around.

I must have delivered my promise, as Debbie crashed out almost instantaneously after climax. She was almost like a man when it came to that. Not once had I received a hard time for not wanting to cuddle afterwards, as she was usually sound asleep, mimicking all sorts of band and farmyard animal impersonations with her talented nostrils. I lay there for a while, but there was no way I was falling asleep with John Deere going full steam ahead, so I decided to put together a plan for the evening.

It was a great brainstorming session, even though I was alone. I did most of my best thinking that way, and really wasn't much of a team player. Ask me that at a job interview though, and you'd hear a completely different story. The strategy for tonight would be to play the homeless card again. I wanted to get close enough to see how large the drug and sex activities were, and that was probably the only way of minimizing trouble. A weekend night should be fairly active if my hunch was correct. Maybe another night I would go down as myself, perhaps bringing Jeff or one of the boys with me for support.

My work for my real job was beginning to suffer. I was due to have a story submitted for the newspaper by five o'clock this evening, and it was after midday already. My motivation was at an all time low, but I had to keep it going until something more prosperous turned up. It was nice being freelance though, no boss bugging me every five minutes, free from the world of corporate bullshit and most of all having the luxury of working from home. If the pay had been better, it would've been an almost perfect set-up. As long as I had it emailed by five o'clock, there wouldn't be any hassles.

I decided to go with my take on customer service at fast food joints, and how the impact of minimum wage work had resulted in a lack of job pride, and in turn little regard for the customer always being right. I included some fictitious references of recent visits to such places, where my order had been messed up, was greeted by rude and obnoxious workers and had a poor customer experience across the board. They would never know I'd made it up, it could never be proved. I'm not even sure if they cared, as long as they got a story to fill up their already scantily filled publication. As much as the article was fabricated, it was definitely a true reflection of society today.

I entered the park, wondering what events were in store this evening. Debbie was still sleeping when I'd left, she must have been really wiped out from her shift last night. Either that or I was just a fantastic lover. I tried to convince myself it was the latter, but deep down I knew that was a bunch of crap.

The restroom appeared to be quiet as I approached. It was only around eight o'clock, and I'd hoped to get into position before anything started to happen. As I walked in, I was more than a little surprised to see Gibby and Dano hanging around the sink area snorting some cocaine. They must've been equally startled, as Gibby almost sucked the entire rolled up dollar bill up his nose.

"Holy fuck, you scared the shit out of me man," he said in his usual polite fashion.

"Here again, don't have a home to go to or something," said Dano, as they both laughed in appreciation at his remark.

I smirked out of politeness, as I didn't want to get on the bad side of these two thugs. I sat in my corner and discreetly reached into my pocket to start recording.

"Needing any drugs?"

"No man, I need a home though, got one of those instead?"

It was a good reply, which they both enjoyed, much to my delight.

"At least you've got a sense of humor man, not like a lot of these other homeless fuckers. I've got some heroin here, real cheap and you'll forget you don't have a home in no time."

"No thanks chief, I don't even have enough money for food. Just had a half eaten sandwich someone had dumped in the trash."

"Fuck dude, that sucks," said Dano, almost apologetically.

My plan was working. If I could get to know these guys to some degree, they wouldn't see me as a threat and maybe I could get some good information out of them as a result.

"So what happened to make you homeless?"

I'd had my story rehearsed in my head for a while, but now it was lights, camera and action time.

"Gambling."

"What sort of gambling?"

"Everything. Horses, football, slot machines, if I could put a bet on something I would. It was like a drug to me and I lost everything. I would've put a

bet on how many sheets of toilet paper it would take to wipe my ass if somebody had given me decent odds."

"Don't go making that bet in this place, chances are the right answer would
be none. There's never any fucking paper in this place, believe me," said Gibby.

He had no idea I was aware of his recent incident, even though I'd been
there.

"I won't be making any more bets, that's for sure. Not only did it cost me my
home, I lost my wife and kids as well. I don't even know where they are right
now."

The sympathy card was always a good one. It was as if they almost felt my
pain, and I was confident that Gibby wouldn't be talking to me like I was a
piece of trash any more.

"Shit man, that's rough."

"So what are you guys hanging around here for at the weekend? Thought a
couple of young men like yourselves would be in town chasing some pussy or
something."

"Maybe later, got a bit of business to take care of. Probably be out of here by
midnight, after we finish doing some deals with the dirty hookers and those
fucking sausage smugglers. I fucking hate those bastards as well, I'd love to give
them a good fucking beating, but I use this place so much and don't want the
Pigs to have an excuse for showing up. They never come around here much
though, probably too much other shit going on in town and I wanna keep it
that way."

Gibby and Dano probably had a few concealed homosexual thoughts, especially with them hanging around here as often. I personally didn't care less if
someone was straight, gay, bisexual or stuck their dick in melons. I was comfortable with my sexuality, and whatever people did in their private lives was
their prerogative. As long as they were happy and didn't force it on me, then I
was cool with it. I just found women absolutely beautiful, especially with them
coming in all different shapes and sizes, each having their own attractive qual-
ities. How a man could find another guy's hairy ass an appealing feature was
beyond me, but to some, this was as appetizing as the dessert cart showing up.
Each to their own though, and whatever made people content with their lives
was the main thing.

"So how's business?" I asked carefully. I didn't want to appear as if I was
snooping, but they'd inquired about me first, so it seemed like a good opportunity to avoid suspicion.

"Never better, a lot of easy picking down here."

"How so?"

"You've seen the types around here. The hookers are pretty much all crack heads, and most of the closet ass bandits want to be a little fucked up before they stick their dick down someone's throat. Not sure why though, but who cares right, all money in my pocket," voiced Gibby.

"It probably makes them feel less guilty when they go home to their wives, mentally blaming the fact they were fucked up at the time, or using it as a way to block out the deceit while they're getting one in the pooper."

"Never thought of it like that. You're pretty smart for a homeless dude," said Dano, looking genuinely impressed.

"Being homeless doesn't automatically mean stupid."

"I know man, just most of you guys that hang around the park are not the brightest bulbs in the box. You're like Alfred Einstein compared to them."

Unless Albert had a genius of a brother I didn't know about, Dano was actually one of the bulbs he was referring to. I was about to respond, but the boys were distracted by some sounds from outside.

"Business is calling," said Gibby as the both walked outside.

They returned in no more than sixty seconds with what were obviously two prostitutes, one of whom was the kind girl with the big hair and boots from the other day.

"Hey stranger," she said to me as they walked back to the sink area.

Gibby handed a small package to the unfamiliar girl and she parted with what looked like a twenty-dollar bill, but I couldn't be sure. He was about to give the same to big hair and boots girl, but stopped at the last minute.

"Aren't we missing something sweetheart?"

"I haven't made any money yet."

"Well you know the drill."

He handed her the package, and they both went into the end cubicle.

"I'll suck it without a condom, but you're not screwing me without one, I don't know where you've been."

At least she used protection, although why there was a difference in her standards between penetration and oral slightly confused me. As for not knowing where Gibby had been, I was quite sure she'd visited a few more nasty "places" than the young drug dealer, which he obviously agreed with.

"Fuck you bitch. Where I've been, you've probably had half the cocks in town in every hole you've got. Just bend over and be quiet, I wouldn't bang you without a rubber even if I was using a fake dick.

Not surprisingly, she had no witty reply for that, other than uttering the word "asshole". The sound of his pelvis area slapping against her ass echoed rhythmically across the room. Dano and the other hooker were doing some coke, and appeared completely uninterested in the other two. Perhaps it was a frequent event now, and the initial novelty had worn off. Not for me though as I was actually getting a little horny.

"Take that you bitch," Gibby was saying, obviously spanking her butt cheeks at the time.

The entire situation and location was so dirty and nasty that it only added to my arousal. Gibby though, didn't do much better than the last client I'd seen the hooker with. Two minutes of hard pounding and ass slapping later, and he let out a huge climax, resembling the howl of a wolf on a full moon night. It was a bit over the top, but comical at the same time, however, the visual image was enough to bring my semi-erect penis back to its original limp state. They came back out and Dano gave Gibby a casual high five, and the girls went on their way.

"That's another reason I hangout here," said Gibby, looking extremely happy with himself.

His obvious glee was a bit surprising in light of his mediocre performance, but in all fairness, appearing as a sensitive and caring lover was likely the last thing on his mind.

The boys had quite a lucrative business going, as a constant stream of clients came in over the next couple of hours. They were a real mixed bunch as well, mainly your late teenage types looking to add to their alcohol buzz, but also some higher class sounding individuals, likely stocking up for a weekend get together at their penthouse apartments. There were others though who came in and collected packages, but handed over no cash. Gibby meticulously noted down the details, before sending them on their way. It was quite an operation, and seemed like the main distribution center for many lower tier dealers. There was no way that Gibby and Dano were the main players in this outfit, as they didn't have the brains to coordinate such a venture. They had to be working for someone much larger in social stature, sitting back and enjoying the majority of the cash flow, while pushing the risk onto these two unsuspecting characters. I tried to capture as many of the conversations as I possibly could, but it was getting tricky. I had ninety minutes worth of tape, and had to discreetly stop and start to ensure gathering as much meaningful material as possible.

Another two guys entered, looking rather wary. They spoke in a very feminine manner to the boys, exchanged money for drugs and headed into one of the stalls.

"Well that's our cue to get the hell outta here," said Dano.

"Yeah, I'm not sticking around to listen to these ass bandits," said Gibby, without any regard to whether the two gentlemen heard him or not. "Need to head into town anyway to get some real pussy," he said, giving me a wink.

"It was nice talking to you boys, take it easy and I'll no doubt run into you again."

"Yeah, same to you dude. Listen, if you ever need to make some cash, we can talk the next time. I might be able to get you running a few errands for me. Might give you a chance to get back on your feet again."

"Thanks man, I'll think about it. I appreciate the thought."

There was no way I would take him up on any offer, but it did make me think about how easy it would be to get some extra money, and in real life, Debbie and myself could certainly use it. The legal implications however, quickly halted any thoughts of accepting.

The gentlemen were in process of snorting down their cocaine, but fortunately no sexual activity had commenced. I was about to call it a night, when four really shady guys wearing matching leather jackets and shaved heads burst in. They were extremely menacing looking and headed straight for the stalls, kicking the door in of the one currently occupied. There was a shriek of terror from inside the cubicle.

"You dirty fuckers," shouted the ringleader of the skinheads.

"Leave us along, we're not doing any harm," cried one of the gay guys.

That was the last of the talking. I was horrified that such hatred still existed in society today. The guys were correct, as they were doing no harm. It wasn't my cup of tea, but each to their own. The two men were dragged out and beaten senseless by the four assholes. They shouted anti-gay statements as they showered punches and kicks down on their squirming bodies. I really felt badly for them, but there was nothing I could do. Any intervention as this point would only have led to three people being beaten as opposed to two. The one guy with his pants around his ankles was even singled out for extra treatment. The struggling continued until they wriggled no more. It was a hate crime beyond any proportion I'd seen before, and it was going to take me some time before I got over the horror of it all. I'd contemplated running away, but was worried they would pursue me and do them same, so I stayed as still and quiet as possible and tried to appear as disinterested as I could. As the dickheads fled the scene, they gave me a quick look, but continued on their way.

"You guys OK?" I asked with genuine concern.

There were a few groans, but that was about all. They were at least alive, but in really bad shape. I stood over their bloodied bodies and surveyed their injuries. Should I go and call the cops? I probably should've, but my own self-ishness stopped me from doing anything rash. I wanted to help them to their feet, but didn't want to chance getting any blood on my hands. In today's world, you just never knew who was carrying a disease. This decision was nothing to do with them being gay, as I would've acted the same had it been a loving young heterosexual couple.

I hung around for a while and eventually they sat up, definitely in shock, but they were going to make it. I didn't want the cops involved as I had my story to complete and this had added a whole new avenue to any article.

"You'd better get yourselves to the Emergency Room guys, you're going to need some stitches at the very least."

They were both sobbing and I couldn't blame them, as the attack was completely unprovoked and no doubt the last thing they'd been expecting. I didn't know what circumstance had brought them here, whether they were sneaking off behind someone's back or just a pair of guys in love, who'd decided to try something a little different from their normal indoor fun. That was unimportant, but they did require medical attention, and the sooner the better.

"Why would they do that? Why?" said the younger guy, pulling up his pants in the process.

"They're just hooligans, think you were just in the wrong place at the wrong time," I lied. They had targeted the fact they were gay, but it may or may not have been coincidental. The thugs may have known it was a hangout for gay men, and our unfortunate victims just happened to be there, or maybe they'd been followed here and it wasn't a random act after all. This I would never know. They both got to their feet, although still extremely wobbly.

"You're going to go and get checked out at the hospital, right?"

"I think we might be OK."

"Come on guys, you've both got some serious gashes that really need stitching. You're losing quite a lot of blood."

I wasn't kidding either, their faces were beaten like the loser in a one sided boxing match. They reluctantly agreed and we headed outside, all carefully checking for any sign of the Nazi boys.

I proceeded off in the opposite direction from the wounded victims. The choice of going to the hospital was in their hands now, there was nothing more I could do other than take them there, but I wanted no part of the outcome. If we had crossed paths with any police officers, they would've been sure to question us in light of their injuries, and I didn't want involved with that or any of the complications it might throw my way.

9

Day Off

After yesterday's events it was time for a day off from hanging out at the park. I had an article to submit for the newspaper anyway, and was shit out of ideas on that front. All focus right now was on my undercover work, and if I wasn't careful, I could be putting my employment in jeopardy.

Debbie wasn't home, so instead of working on my piece for the paper, I figured some 'fun for one' would be as relaxing as anything. I got situated with my box of tissues, tube of lotion and switched on the TV, as one of the cable channels was certain to have some tacky porn movie playing. I was psyched up and ready to go, only to discover there was no visible picture on any of the channels. That wasn't completely true, but the quality was so bad it would've been as well being a blank screen. The porn channel was awful. I could just about decipher a nipple, but nowhere near enough to enable a pleasurable experience, so decided to call the cable company.

I'd been on hold for about fifteen minutes and almost ready to hang up, when a young sounding female with a foreign accent finally answered.

"Hello, thees eez Liliana."

"Hi Liliana, I'm calling regarding my cable service. I'm looking at my TV screen right now and the picture quality is extremely bad."

"OK, youz can steel see screen, yes?"

"Yes, I am looking at the screen, but the picture quality is very bad and all channels are unwatchable."

"Peecture ith very bad," she said in fluent Spanglish.

"Yes, peecture ith very bad. Need someone to come feex peecture, yes?" I replied, praying for a better response if I mimicked her accent. This was unbelievable. I felt like I was stranded all alone, somewhere in continental Europe, not in my own living room in the United States of America.

"OK, one momento pleez."

I was back on hold again. How difficult could it be to schedule someone to come out and repair? Even my finest pigeon English had caused her confusion. So much for thinking it would have accelerated the proceedings.

"Hello, can I help you?"

Who the fuck was this now? I hated being passed over to someone else as it meant explaining the whole deal again.

"Hi, I was just explaining to your Foreign colleague that my picture quality is very poor."

"Would you mind holding for one minute please?"

"Actually I would, I was holding for fifteen minutes before finally speaking to Liliana, who may I add, had about as much grasp of the English language as a rural Chinese homeless person, and now I'm having to explain everything again, and now *you* want to put me on hold *again*!"

"There's no need for the attitude sir."

"I'm not giving you an attitude, I just don't appreciate being given the runaround. Whatever happened to looking out for the customer's needs?"

"Well sir, maybe if you relax a little I'll be willing to assist you."

"Excuse me, but do you know who you are talking to?"

"Do you know who you are talking to sir?"

"No."

"Sweet."

The phone went dead. The little prick had hung up on me. I was absolutely flabbergasted. What the hell was wrong with the world today? You pay for a service, but as soon as anything goes wrong, you need to endure a conversation with either a foreign retard or some smartass piece of shit who really couldn't give a crap. I was fuming, but resisted phoning back as I'd probably only make matters worse. Even if I'd got through to someone nice, I'd have taken my rage out on them and that wasn't fair. The one positive from it all was giving me an idea for my article. Why I hadn't thought of it sooner only informed me that I wasn't exactly on the ball either. The story would be a follow-up to my previous slant on customer service of fast food restaurants. This time the focus would be on call centers and how customer care was almost an after thought. It really pissed me off to have to spend five minutes going through a series of automated options that more often than not, excluded the opportunity of actually speaking to a person. Even after stumbling on this choice—after several previous menus of irrelevant crap—it usually meant waiting in line until somebody could be bothered answering, and when they did, it was usually just the beginning of more problems. It was an easy article to write as it came from the heart, and I had it wrapped up and emailed to the editor within an hour.

With the TV out of action for now, I got back down to planning the remainder of my restroom exploits. I felt I almost had enough information to create something of substance, with just a few finishing touches required before I could get back to a normal daily life.

I put on my Jerry Mitchell CD and sat down at the kitchen table with my notebook. For some reason I could always think more clearly with music playing, especially with Jerry's songs, even though I hated the asshole.

The one thing missing from my work so far was photographs. If I was contemplating a successful multi episode national newspaper story, it was one thing to have the audio evidence of the drug exchanges and sexual encounters, but for the viewing public, photographic evidence was a must, even if I had to airbrush out the faces for legal reasons. That was going to be a tricky one though. I was confident of discreetly concealing my digital camera, but much of the action seemed to occur at night, and it was pretty dimly lit inside the bathroom. There was no way I could get away with using a flash, so I had to hope there would be some daytime activity. We would find out tomorrow afternoon.

I must have dozed off for a while, as the sound of the front door opening caused me to jump into action, briefly unaware of my surroundings or what time of day it was. I was expecting Debbie, but there were a few voices. Was someone breaking into my apartment? I grabbed the rolling pin from the kitchen drawer and quietly tiptoed my way towards the front door.

Debbie, Jeff and Graeme burst into laughter as I stood before them yielding the rolling pin.

"You scared the shit outta me," I said genuinely, as they continued to laugh.

"What were you going to do, roll me to death," replied big Graeme.

"Fuck you, I wasn't expecting you all. Better safe than sorry."

"I'm just glad you pulled up your pants from around you're ankles before confronting us," said Jeff, jumping on the ball busting wagon.

"I don't know Jeff, we might have been more scared if he'd come through holding *that* weapon in his hand instead."

"Thanks honey, I'll take that as a compliment."

"So how's it going Inspector Clouseau?" inquired Jeff in a sarcastic tone.

"Pretty good actually. I'm thinking about wrapping the story up in the next day or two. You'd be amazed at the number of weird and wonderful characters that hang around there. Fuck, last night I even witnessed two homosexual guys get the living shit beaten out of them. They were just minding their own business as well, as a gang of Nazi looking pricks with their shaved heads came in, busted into the cubicle the two guys were in and proceeded to knock seven shades of shit out of them."

"I'm glad you're finishing this up soon, I really worry when you tell me stuff like that," said my little sweetheart.

"Yeah, you really need to watch yourself chief, sounds like some crazy assed stuff."

"Tell me about it. I'm heading back there tomorrow though. You boys should come along and check it out."

"What do you think Jeff?" said Graeme.

"I'm up for it, might be a laugh."

"It'll be a laugh alright, even if it's just seeing me lying around on a skanky bathroom floor. I'm sure I could even hook you up with one of the fine looking guys that hang around. You'd probably like that Jeff."

"Fuck you Danny, takes one to know one."

"Yeah, I've been getting pounded every day. I'd recommend the Village People biker boy with the twelve incher."

We bullshitted each other for a while longer as we drank and played some poker, but deep down I could tell the guys were looking forward to what lay in store.

10

Weeding Things Out

The doorbell went around eight o'clock. I thought it was a dream, but Debbie elbowed me in the side of the head.

"I'm not answering that," she said in an adamant tone.

I made my way in zombie like fashion to the door.

"Morning chief," said Jeff, sounding way too chipper for this time of the day.

My head was pounding. The last tequila shot last night basically sent me into oblivion. It was like someone was playing punch bag inside my skull as I put on a pot of coffee and strutted around in my boxer shorts.

"You in character right now or are you just fucked up from last night?"

"Totally fucked up. There's no way I can keep up with you alcoholics."

"Practice dude, practice. Even Debbie could kick your ass these days."

He was bullshitting either. She could probably drink me under the table right now, which was sad, but I didn't care. I had more important things on my mind, like finishing up this story.

"Yeah whatever, let's just get some coffee in us and get on our way."

"Well, let's see you in your outfit."

I got dressed and came back through to the living room.

"Holy fuck dude, I feel like I should be giving you some spare change."

"That's the idea you dumb fuck."

"I just hope you gave those jeans a wash after lying around in all that shit."

"Not at all. I'm not supposed to smell like washing detergent you retard."

"Well your plan is definitely working, you look and smell like dog crap."

"As long as I'm convincing."

"More than that buddy, I'm actually starting to feel sorry for you, and that'll be a first."

As much as it was degrading, I was glad the desired effect was there. We finished up our coffee and headed for the Subway.

The journey was like an eighth grade school outing, as the boys giggled all the way to the park station. They loved watching people avoid me like the plague and chuckled every time somebody almost sat down beside me, but changed their mind at the last possible minute. Their laughter was like a school kid who'd just let go a huge fart. I knew they would change their attitude after seeing the reality of public bathroom life.

We arrived at the restroom, and as usual it was quiet for this time in the morning. As nothing was going on, the boys headed off to the café for some breakfast and I assumed my position in the corner of the room. As usual, I began to doze off, it had become like a ritual. Voices awakened me, and to no surprise it was Gibby and Dano.

"Morning dude," said Dano a little perturbed he'd woken me.

"How you doing guys?"

"One thousand dollars better off after our visit to the horse racing."

Cock suckers! These guys could fall in the river and come out with fish in their pockets. They were getting away with drug dealing and now they win a fortune at the track. What were the chances? Perhaps the Devil existed after all.

"Congratulations, you're obviously better at the horses than I ever was. Just be careful, it's addictive and will come back and bite you. Don't want you to end up being neighbors of mine right here."

"Yeah, you're right, but we'll enjoy it for now. It's fun once in a while."

Several businessmen funneled in and out, and the boys were making a killing. Who would've thought this would've been a hub for executive drug trading.

Jeff and Graeme finally appeared. I'd already versed them as far as appearing not to know me. I could see a huge smirk on Jeff's face though as he walked past, and they both went over for a piss.

"Another couple of faggots," said Gibby, a little too loudly.

"What the fuck did you say?" said Graeme, turning and giving them a stare as he urinated.

"Nothing dude," replied Dano nervously.

Gibby and Dano were shady characters, but Graeme was just plain intimidating looking, and not shy about displaying it if the situation required.

"Thought you just called me a faggot. Just as well you didn't then, or I'd have to fucking rearrange that pretty boy face of yours."

Gibby was silent, but I could tell that deep down he was fuming. My only concern right now was that he was probably carrying a weapon of some sort, and I was sure he wasn't afraid to use it.

"There's no need to be like that," said Dano.

He knew Gibby was boiling over inside, so was doing his best to diffuse the situation.

"I'm just letting you know. We're not looking for any trouble either boys."

Jeff was squirming a little, but was likely glad it was Graeme who was with him. If anything kicked off, he'd probably not have to lift a fingernail, as Graeme would tear them both a new asshole in just a few seconds.

"You guys dealing?" inquired Graeme, pulling up his zipper.

"No, just hanging out," lied Dano.

"Funny place to be hanging out. Look, we're not cops if that's what you're worried about."

"We might be then. What're you looking for?"

"Just some weed."

As much as he was into fitness, Graeme not only liked his beer, but was partial to the occasional joint. Gibby seemed to relax a little, probably content he'd be making even more cash. I resisted all temptation to snap a shot of Graeme being handed his small bag of weed. I would never use the shot for my story, but it might've been worth the ball busting I could've given him, but I didn't fancy getting a slap around the head.

They were all talking now and seemed to have put the original confrontation behind them. Graeme expertly put a joint together, something I'd never been able to get the hang of. No matter how many times I'd tried, they were always too baggy or I ended up dropping everything on the floor.

"So I hear that some dirty hookers hang out around here," said Graeme in a strange pitch of voice as he inhaled.

"Not at this time of the day," replied Dano, as Graeme passed him the smoke.

"Any hot looking ones?"

"There's one who's pretty sweet. She's got some crazy looking hair, but cute as shit and could suck a tomato through a tennis racket," said Gibby, now relaxed and warming up to the boys.

"Sounds like you've been there chief."

"Once or twice. She likes her weed and coke, and that's her way of paying for it. Pretty good trade if you ask me."

"I might need to check her out."

"You should man, best blow job ever, and cheap as well. Might set you back about forty bucks, but much cheaper than some of these high class massage places, and probably much better. She's here most nights, usually around eight or so."

"Might be the only way you'll get a chick to suck you off big guy," laughed Jeff.

"Fuck you asshole, just never tried it with a professional before. She'll probably give me the money back anyway after seeing my huge hunk of meat," replied Graeme, grabbing his crotch.

They were getting on like a house on fire, and the weed was certainly mellowing everyone out. In a way I hoped Graeme would follow through with the prostitute idea. This was one key photograph I needed, and it would be a great way of achieving my goal if somehow he could get close to her. I couldn't take her photograph, I mean, what would she think about a supposed homeless guy with a digital camera? There was also the fact that she was mainly here at night and I would need to use the flash to guarantee any clarity. I'd needed to make sure he did more than just talk about getting together with her.

11

The Money Shot

The boys and myself arrived back at my place around 2:00pm. They had smoked another joint with Gibby and Dano before heading off. I followed shortly afterwards, telling the dealers I was off down to the duck pond, and I caught up with the guys at the Subway station. Their heads were pretty mashed and they giggled most of the way home.

At home I put on a pot coffee while Jeff and Graeme raided the fridge and kitchen cabinet for any morsel of food they could get their hands on—they had the munchies big time. I sat on the sofa with Jeff, as Graeme slouched in the lazy-boy, giving it its true meaning as he chomped ferociously on a bag of Cheetos.

"So big guy, I could use your help tonight."

"With what?"

"I need to get a shot of the hookers down at the park, but they'll be really suspicious if a homeless dude pulls out a digital camera."

"I suppose so, but can you not just secretly do it yourself?"

"Can't, it'll be dark outside by then and I'll need to use the flash."

"I don't think some hooker is gonna let me take her photograph either. It's not like she's doing something legal. I'm sure she wants to remain as anonymous as possible."

"Maybe you can just snap her quickly and take off before she really knows what's going on?"

"Danny, I'll probably fuck that up and then she'll not be around there again in a while. She'll probably think the cops are onto her or something."

He brought up a good point.

"Don't worry about it then, I'll think of something. Maybe I'll leave it until the end of what I'm doing and take the shot myself."

"Nah dude, I'll help you out, don't want you getting into trouble. She might recognize your face, even if you're dressed in your normal clothes. You hang out down at that duck pond a lot, so I don't want her spotting you sometime down the line and have some crazy pimp dude after your ass."

He brought up another good point that I hadn't even considered.

"Shit, you think pretty well when you're stoned big guy."

"I'll sort you out. I haven't had a blow job in a while, so maybe I'll try out this chick with the mad hair that the boys down there were going on about. If she sucks my cock she might let me take her photograph. Not much chance she'll think I'm a cop after blowing me. I'll tell her it was the best I've ever had and I want a picture so I can jerk off to it at home or something. I'll throw her an extra twenty or something, but who knows, she might do it for free. Might be a nice boost to her ego if a big strapping guy wants to spank his monkey while looking at her."

The guy was a genius. I was waiting on a smart remark from Jeff, but I turned to find him fast asleep next to me.

"Super idea buddy, I'll pay for your BJ seeing as you're taking one for the team."

"Too right you will. It's going to be such a hardship dumping a load in a dirty chick's mouth. The things I do for you."

He was a funny guy. He was seriously helping me out, but he might end up getting a free blowjob so I didn't feel too bad.

"We can head down around nine o'clock if that works for you?"

"Sounds cool, I don't have anywhere I need to be. I think Jeff has the right idea, might join him for a quick nap. Wake me up in a little bit."

No sooner had he finished his sentence, he began to snore, but nothing in comparison to my tractor wife. The weed must've been good stuff, as it had knocked them both on their ass.

"Wakey wakey boys," I shouted, both of them almost jumping to attention like a couple of nervous soldiers.

"What the fuck dude, where's the fire?" whined Jeff.

"You've been sleeping for about three hours you couple of lazy bastards."

"You're kidding me."

"Check your watch if you don't believe me."

Graeme started to chuckle.

"What the fuck's so funny?" asked Jeff, chuckling to himself also.

"Nothing, still a bit stoned I think."

Jeff made his way through to the bathroom, probably to give his face a wash and waken up.

"YOU FUCKING LITTLE PRICK," came the shout from Jeff, as Graeme and I roared with laughter.

While he'd been asleep, I'd decided to give him a full makeover using some of Debbie's lipstick and mascara. I just wish I'd been there to see the look on his face in the mirror. He came back though, all cleaned up.

"Nice one Danny, you dickhead. Shit, I never even felt a thing, I must've been really out of it."

"You were you lightweight. You were well out of it as soon as your ass hit the couch. Nice one Danny. Stick on some coffee, I'll be back in a minute, I'm bursting for a piss. Feels like my back teeth are floating," said Graeme heading through to the restroom.

"YOU ASSHOLE," screamed Graeme, but we could hear his laughter, which was replicated only louder by Jeff and myself.

"AT FIRST I THOUGHT IT WAS JUST YOU AS WELL," roared Jeff.

"On a roll today aren't we," exclaimed Graeme, as I handed him a well-earned coffee.

"I just couldn't resist it."

"We'll get revenge you little penis, you can be sure about that."

I had no doubt that would be true.

Graeme and myself headed back down to the park around 8:30pm. Jeff had left earlier as he was working a night shift.

"You nervous?" I asked.

"About what?"

"About getting together with a hooker."

"Hell no, a blow job's a blow job. Just keep your eye out for any cops, the last thing I need is to get busted."

"No worries dude. I haven't seen a cop since I've been going down here, but I'll keep watch just in case."

"Have you seen this broad those dealers were talking about?"

"Yeah, a few times. She's really cute actually, I'd give her one."

"Like that tells me a lot, you'd stick your dick in a hairy donut you dirty little bastard."

"Maybe a long time ago, but Debbie's the only one for me now."

"Yeah, you've got a little gem there chief. I really need to get my act together and find a decent woman myself. I'm a little fed up with these airheads I seem to end up with."

"It'll find you when you least expect it."

"So they tell me, just wish it would hurry up and happen. The one-night stands are getting a bit dull. The last couple of times have been shit. Both were happy taking, but not a lot of giving, especially that last one, the Latin looking girl. I must have been down on her for about half an hour. I almost needed a fucking oxygen tank I was that out of breath. Afterwards my tongue felt like I'd been licking stamps for about a week. Did she return the favor, did she fuck. She was happy to lie back though while I pounded her. Crap though, it was like banging a statue, must've worn her out with all the oral."

"Never even sucked you off, I hate chicks like that. They'd be the first to complain if the tables were reversed."

"Exactly, that's why I'm looking forward to this tonight, no messing around. Tell her what you want, hand her some cash and off we go. I'd spend more on a dinner date, and with the way my luck is going right now I wouldn't get blown, so this is almost perfect."

He made yet another good point. A night on the town with a girl would be way more expensive, without the guarantee of any action. What harm did paying for it really cause anyway? That's one of the reasons I was against prostitution being illegal. In the grand scheme of crime in the world, was that really such a big deal? I'd much rather any police resource was put into catching burglars, rapists and murderers, not busting some young desperate single mother who's just trying to feed her family, or the ugly loner of a guy using her services who isn't able to get a real girlfriend. I mean, give these guys a break. Let them indulge in some sexual activity that doesn't involve a large piece of fruit or their own hand for a change. Built up sexual frustration is sometimes enough to drive these social outcasts crazy.

"Well I'm sure you'll enjoy. I'm almost positive she'll be around."

"Better be, I'm really starting to get horny now with all this sex talk."

As I predicted, she was standing outside the restroom. We were well out of range, but I could make out the big hair.

"Right, you know what to do," I said, handing Graeme the camera.

"Sure, pull out my dick and stick it in her mouth."

"You know what I mean you sarcastic prick."

"I've got it covered."

He headed off and I hung back for about 30 seconds. I approached just in time to see them both heading into the ladies room. In a strange, almost perverted way, I stood around outside the ladies entrance hoping to hear what was going on. Even if it was just to get a few words from Graeme that I could wind him up about the next time we were in the bar with the boys.

"Holy shit, I didn't know they still made them that big," I heard her gasp.

I was a little envious of the big man. He was hung like a horse, and from what I'd heard from some of the skanks he'd been with, he knew how to use it as well.

"They don't, I'm just unique," said the cocky bastard.

"If I'd known this before you parted with the money I might have given you a discount. This thirty dollars is looking like about three dollars an inch."

"Yeah, it's about ten inches."

"Just hope I can get my mouth around it."

Son of a bitch, mine wouldn't even be ten inches if my starting point was sticking the measuring tape in my butthole!

All was quiet for a while, other than the occasional groan from Graeme. He was doing a lot better than most of the two-minute men who regularly used her services.

"Don't come yet, I want to feel that thing inside my pussy."

"I don't have much more money with me."

"Keep your money, I haven't had one like that for a long time."

Unbelievable it was. Here was me looking for some good material to bring up at the bar, but I was getting nothing. If anything it was actually the other way around. I could just see him happily letting everyone know he got a free screw from a hooker because he had such a huge tool. The groaning was louder now, but it wasn't coming from Graeme—she was loving every minute of it. Finally there was a huge mutual groan. Not only did he get a free shag, but finished it off with a simultaneous orgasm, and I could tell she wasn't faking it either.

I heard them making their way out, so I sat on the ground appearing none the wiser of what had just taken place. He had a confident strut to him and she was walking like she'd just lost her donkey.

"That was great, thanks sweetheart."

"No thank you, make sure you come back here again. You're money is no good here," she said giving him a sexy wink.

"Won't be back for a while, heading out of town for a couple of weeks, I'm a freelance photographer."

"Sounds very exciting, maybe I can get you to take some sexy shots of me sometime?"

Credit where credit's due, he was playing this like he was up for a major part in a motion picture.

"Now you mention it, any chance I can take one of you now?"

"With my clothes on?"

"Yeah, absolutely. I've got your naked body etched in my mind forever. As I said, I'm going out of town and not going to have much free time to relax. Was hoping I could get a photograph of you to take with me. It'll give me something to jerk off to on the lonely nights."

"Well if you put it like that, why not. As long as you promise to come back sometime and give me a workout like that again."

"You've got a deal, just give me a sexy pose."

He was even acting like he was really a photographer, and she was buying every word of it. He must've taken about ten pictures and I'd only been expecting one if I was lucky.

"That's it gorgeous, work it. Beautiful, I almost feel like jerking off right now."

"You really are something boy."

"Anyway sweetheart, I need to get going. I'll see you in a couple of weeks."

He bent down and handed me a dollar.

"Here you go dude, you look like you need this more than me."

He had his back to her and he stared at me, his eyes wide and tongue flicking in and out. He was such a dick, but a lovable one at that.

"That was really nice of you," she said.

It was almost like I wasn't there. He kissed her on the cheek and headed on his way.

"Wow," she said out loud.

"Take it you're having a good night?" I asked.

"I was, but it can only go downhill from here."

Graeme was waiting for me at the Subway Station with a massive smirk on his face.

"I can only assume it was everything you wanted it to be."

"That would be the understatement of the year, she was unbelievable. Really got into it and was surprisingly tight for a hooker."

"Come on horse cock, the top of a bucket would be a tight squeeze for you."

"You make a fine point pencil dick."

"You going to pay her a visit again then?"

"I might just do that," he said with a grin, and handed me the camera.

12

A Picture's Worth a Thousand Words

I sat in my familiar corner of the restroom and contemplated. This was definitely my last day. The last week had been an interesting experience to say the least. I just wanted a few more photos of some drug dealing and perhaps some homosexual interaction to wrap things up. My respect for the homeless had changed significantly. Having to hang around festering places like this to keep out of the rain and be exposed to as many shady characters wasn't a pleasant experience. As little wealth as I had in this world, I was a millionaire in their eyes, so I couldn't really complain about my situation, even though it was far from what I'd envisioned several years ago. Time passed slowly and the activity level was almost non-existent, other than a few passers by outside, but nobody entered the bathroom and I began to drift off.

I was awakened by the familiar voices of Gibby and Dano, as my eyelids opened in slow motion.

"Afternoon," said Dano.

"Hey guys," I replied, with as much enthusiasm as a drunk climbing out of bed in the morning.

I had no idea how long I'd been passed out for, but if it was indeed afternoon, it must've been a couple of hours at least. Realizing why I was here and what the guys would be involved in snapped me back to reality. Now I just had to pick the most opportune moment to snap a shot of a drug exchange and I could get out of here for good.

"Sounds like you had a long night chief," said Gibby, as he pulled a cellophane bag of white powder from his pocket.

"Every night's a long night for me, especially last night. I spent most of it down at the pond. The cock suckers in here last night were keeping me awake and I couldn't take it any longer."

"I hate that shit as well man, it's just not natural if you ask me. If they weren't such good customers for me I'd make sure those fucks never hung around here again."

"I hear you. I should probably start sleeping in the ladies room or something. I don't mind being kept awake by people fucking as long as I know there's some pussy involved."

They got a kick out of that line.

"You're alright dude, I like the way you think. You hungry?"

"Always."

I actually was as I'd skipped breakfast.

"Here, take one of these," said Dano, handing me one of his breakfast burritos.

"Thanks man, appreciate it."

"No worries, you need it more than I do," he said, patting on his beer gut.

These guys weren't all bad. My initial impression was that they were the scum of the earth, but they had some compassion. I didn't condone what they did for a living, but people wanted drugs, and if it didn't come from these guys, there was someone around the corner who would've fixed them up.

It wasn't long before a suit with a briefcase showed up. I was still flabbergasted by how many high-class clients they serviced, but this was perfect, and added a great angle to my story. It wasn't just your low class stereotypical folks who were users, but your yuppie types were rife with it for recreational purposes. I carefully slipped the digital camera from my pocket, one eye on the guys and the other on the power button. It was much easier than I'd anticipated, and the burrito wrapper acted as an excellent shield.

Click, I got the shot. The clarity was great and showed them in mid exchange. It was back in my pocket in a heartbeat and nobody was any the wiser. I was so glad it was daytime and didn't have to fuck around with the flash.

"Wow, that burrito really cheered you up," said Dano.

I must've had a slight grin on my face, but obviously due to my photograph accomplishment, rather than the satisfaction of a hearty breakfast.

"Absolutely, totally hit the spot. Thanks again, kicks the ass off any sandwich that's been marinating in a garbage can."

"Not a problem dude. Anyway, take it easy, we're outta here. That douche bag just fixed us up with enough cash to last a week. These business fools pay crazy money for what we give them. Going to head down to the race track for a while and see if we can make some more."

"OK guys, take it easy with the horses. Remember what I said before, you don't want to end up sitting here with me one of these days."

"You're a funny dude man, later."

Off they went as happy as a couple of pigs in shit. They weren't alone, a quick piss and I was out of here as well.

There is an unwritten rule known to many as public pissing etiquette, which was being violated to the n-th degree. There were four urinals side by side in the restroom, and I had occupied the end unit. A guy had came in who'd obviously missed the training class, as he began using the one *directly* next to me, which clearly broke the rule of having to use the opposite end if only two people are in the bathroom. I'd been enjoying my well earned pee until this bozo had appeared, but I was now extremely uncomfortable. I contemplated making a comment, but any chit-chat at this precise moment was strictly forbidden also. To my alarm he began whistling the banjo music from the old Burt Reynolds movie Deliverance. I was panicking inside, and had a flashback to the scene of the film where Ned Beatty was raped by the two gross looking Hillbillies. I had to finish this up quickly and get the hell out of here. He was a big guy as well and could've easily overpowered me. I could just visualize being held down, with him shouting 'squeal piggy squeal'. I pushed and squeezed as hard as I could in an attempt to speed up my piss. Unfortunately this caused me to fart, much to the hilarity of this weirdo next to me. I wished it had been a fart, but it wasn't, it was a shart, implying I'd farted and shit my pants at the same time—damn you breakfast burrito. Without a second thought, I whipped my penis midstream, back into my now nasty pants, and bolted out of the place without looking back.

I sat in wait in the surrounding bushes, waiting for the freak to appear which he eventually did. He looked around, but I was well out of sight. What was the deal with this prick? I hung around until he went on his way then headed back into the toilet to clean myself up. This was unbelievable, two shitting incidents since I'd been coming here, but this was the first time I'd actually gone in my pants since being in diapers. There'd better be fucking toilet paper. Fortunately, for a change, there was almost a full roll, which was lucky, as this was going to require more than the usual amount.

I cleaned myself up as best as I could, and as before, decided the underwear wasn't salvageable, which was fine, as I was wearing a three dollar pair from Target and not my Calvin Klein's.

There was the sound of a couple of guys entering the restroom, and no doubt drug use or oral sex was on their agenda, which was standard procedure for this place. Something sounded strangely familiar with one of them, but I couldn't put my finger on it. The more I racked my brain the more it was irritating me, as I knew this voice. I was puzzled, as I didn't know many gay people, but from the conversation they were engaged in, they most definitely were.

"Just give *me* a blow job, but I don't have time to suck yours," said the familiar voice.

"Great, that sounds good to me—not!"

"You can jerk off after I'm gone. My God, you're such a fucking queen."

"I just don't think it's fair, it should be give *and* take."

"I'll call the fucking shots. If you knew who I was you wouldn't be giving me any of your fairy bullshit."

Right then it hit me, and as quiet as I was being I could hardly contain myself, as I'd just hit the jackpot. I was almost positive it was the voice of Jerry Mitchell. Maybe I was mistaken, but this guy was a complete asshole, just as Jerry had been to me all those years ago. Well today he was going to face the pain.

"Just get it in your fucking mouth," I heard him say.

Shit, this other guy really didn't mind being treated like crap, probably a fetish of some variety. They were three cubicles away, so I got my head down to the floor as far as possible, being careful not to get shit on my face. I could see their feet, but was essentially oblivious to fact the other guy was on his knees—an act that would've usually grossed me out. It *was* Jerry fucking Mitchell, there was no doubt in my mind. He'd always worn cowboy style boots, and right there, almost winking at me, were a shiny black leather pair, the gleam from the silver buckle matching my beaming smile of delight. Well this prick wouldn't be smiling in just a few minutes.

"Faster you little bitch," ordered Jerry.

I really had to get on this one fast, as opportunities like this didn't present themselves everyday. It was a race against ejaculation, as I slipped like an assassin into the adjacent stall, holding my camera like a high tech handgun. I carefully and silently stood on the toilet bowl and peered over the top of the wall. It was Jerry alright, with his little slave's head going back and forth like a fiddler's elbow. I switched on the camera flash. I only had one shot at this, and didn't care about being detected, just as long as the photograph was a good one, that was the main objective.

They were in the center of the frame, and Jerry's face was the only missing component. I loudly cleared my throat and watched as Jerry turned towards me. It seemed like slow motion as his startled look turned to horror.

"SMILE MOTHER FUCKER," I shouted, pulling the trigger.

Immediately I bailed out, way faster than Jerry, as I heard him scrambling madly to get out. He was fighting a losing battle, as I wasn't the one with a set of teeth around my dick. If he wasn't careful he could get a nasty flesh wound, but right now that was the least of his problems.

"COME BACK HERE YOU PIECE OF SHIT," I heard him scream.

It was very faint though as I was running like a greyhound, and didn't plan on stopping anytime soon.

I almost puked as I reached the Subway station, but breathed deeply as I waited on the next train, which eased the nausea.

I got onto the train and sat back, delighted by the accomplishments of the day. No sooner had I started to relax, my pulse rocketed into overdrive. Running towards the open door was Jerry Mitchell like a possessed cowboy— he looked desperate. His career and reputation had probably flashed through his mind like the camera in the bathroom. I got up, but was rooted to the spot with panic. The doors began to close in what again seemed like slow motion. They closed not a moment too soon as he screeched in pain, his fingers stuck in the door. He jolted back, which was just as well for me, as the door finally closed firmly behind him and the train set off on its way. He chased to no avail, shouting and screaming at me in rage as I stared into his demonic eyes. I laughed in his face, revenge was sweet. I aimed the camera and snapped a perfect shot of him again, which captured his anger flawlessly. This would only compliment the one of him with his cock in the young guy's mouth.

They say a picture's worth a thousand words. Well, one thing was for sure, these pictures were going to be worth a hell of a lot more than I'd ever make from selling my restroom article.

Burning with Silence

Burning with Silence

1

Phantom of the Opera

It'd been six months since the accident and I wasn't dealing with the outcome very well. Therapy had helped a little, but I didn't like exposing myself to a stranger, so I quit. It was time to face the world again—that would be my real therapy. What the hell was post-traumatic stress disorder anyway? I loathed the way my therapist referred to it as PTSD and assumed I knew what it meant. In my case it was apparently some kind of psychiatric disorder as a result of my accident. She said there was a good chance that my trauma would go away over time, but there was a possibility I could have stressful reactions that would prevent that or in fact make it even worse. It *was* getting worse, and the more sessions I had with her were only adding to my stress. It was probably my doing, but I couldn't bring myself to open up to her.

I'd never been well liked, even as a child. Why I felt the need to conceal my childhood issues from the therapist was beyond me. Maybe I didn't want to expose any potential red flags. My early anger and violence issues were surely a thing of the past, but I didn't need them entering my mind again, especially now.

I just needed to jump back on the horse. Like a new haircut, people notice a difference at first, get used to the change and stop talking about it. They would likely go back to treating me as they did before, or so I hoped. Nobody liked me, but I was fine with that. Business was business, and I wasn't there to make friends.

My life before the accident had been in shreds. I loved my wife and kids, but the feeling wasn't mutual, especially from my wife's perspective. I'd treated her badly and was now paying the consequences. When they moved out I started to spiral even further down the staircase of unhappiness. I hadn't seen or heard from them in over a year and had no idea where they were, so assumed they were gone for good. Why I'd thought alcohol was the answer remained a mystery, but the evening of the accident would haunt me forever.

It was one night when I was home alone, feeling sorry for myself and working my way through a bottle of Scotch like drinking was being outlawed the following day. I could feel myself getting sleepier by the sip, but continued on unperturbed. I didn't usually smoke inside the house, but didn't give a shit anymore. The kids weren't around, so I didn't need to hide the fact. The more I reflected, the sleepier I became, and I must've passed out almost coma like into a dream, which became the biggest nightmare imaginable.

I was awakened by an extreme burning sensation—I was on fire. As drunk as I was, the sobering effect was unbelievable. The armchair and my clothes were in flames and I was in a panic like I'd never experienced before. I couldn't think straight, but any delays in my actions would only lead to further damage. I tried to put out the fire on the chair, but the pain was excruciating. I rolled around on the floor, but it was no use. I darted outside to the patio area and jumped into the pool. The relief was astonishing, but there was no time for complacency. I charged back into the house and grabbed the mini fire extinguisher. The fire alarms were going crazy and probably had been for some time. There wasn't a moment to lose. I let loose with the extinguisher, and fortunately managed to control the flames, collapsing onto the floor as the last of the fire was quenched. I sat in disbelief before finally calling 911. I needed to get to the emergency room quickly. I knew smoking was bad for me, but always thought the cancer aspect was the danger, and never envisioned it would be the cause of such an accident.

As I lay in the ambulance on the way to the hospital I started to sob. What had become of my life? I was a mess and it was all my doing. Maybe this was God's way of paying me back for being such an asshole over the years.

The paramedics were treating my injuries as carefully as possible, but the pain was verging on unbearable and I must've been in shock. They had removed my clothing and were applying some kind of cream to the affected areas. My entire right side was stinging, but my face appeared to be their main concern. The vision in my right eye was blurred to say the least, but I hoped it was just a result of the treatment applied. I couldn't tell how bad things were, but from their levels of anxiety I knew it wasn't pretty.

2

Burns of the Third Degree

I was awakened by the nurse and a distinguished looking grey haired gentleman, who I assumed was a Doctor of some sort. My recollection of the previous night was minimal. The fire itself would be etched in my memory forever, and I could recall parts of the ambulance ride, but other than that the rest was a mystery.

"How are you feeling Mr. McKenzie?" inquired the Doctor, with a sympathetic tone.

"Where am I Doctor?"

"You're in the burns unit. You've been through quite an ordeal and we're going to have to do some skin grafting surgery on you in order to correct some of the disfigurement."

"Disfigurement?"

The word itself was terrifying and my panic escalated out of control.

"Mr. McKenzie, you've suffered third degree burns on your abdomen, arm and also your face."

"Get me a mirror, get me a fucking mirror!"

"Calm down sir, you're in the best possible place right now and we will do everything in our power to reconstruct your appearance."

"Please get me a mirror," I sobbed.

The nurse scurried off after the Doctor gave her a quick nod.

"I can understand your trauma right now Mr. McKenzie, I really can. I see these injuries every other day, and your current reaction is very common. Most people have a completely different view after surgery, and I'm sure you'll feel the same. Just give it time."

"Just get me mirror, *please*."

The nurse returned with a large mirror in a wooden frame. It looked like she'd removed it from an office wall or something. She reluctantly handed it to me with a concerned look on her face.

Nothing on this earth could've prepared me for what I was about to see.

"NO NO NO," I screamed, before bursting into a mixture of rage and sheer panic. It was beyond bad, and appeared as though someone had taken a blow-torch to the right side of my face. It was completely melted away and I was like the Phantom from the Andrew Lloyd Webber musical. I just wanted to die. My life was worthless anyway, so why fucking bother. The surgeon needed to be a genius to correct this, but I just couldn't see it happening.

"Mr. McKenzie, I understand your pain, but let us do our work and make this as better as possible. Medical advancements have come a long way in treating burn injuries."

"I want to be left alone right now."

"I understand, but please try and remain positive. I know it's tough right now, but you are in the best of care."

"Please just leave. I need to think and try to come to terms with this."

They went on their way and I started to cry.

3

Success My Ass

I checked myself and heavily bandaged face out of the hospital. According to the surgeon the operation had been "a complete success". Fuck those assholes. I'd decide the rating on the success scale, not them. I nervously headed on my way, back home, back to the scene of the accident.

As I entered the house, the charcoal like smell was very evident, causing a horrible flashback to the night I'd never forget. My heart pumped and again tears filled my eyes. I wasn't usually a very expressive person, unless you count being angry with work colleagues, but crying had never been part of my emotional composition—except when it concerned my late Father. Over the last day or so however, I hadn't been able to control myself. I tried to fight it, but it was like a lightweight taking on a heavyweight for the title, there was no way of winning the battle. There was more to it than just the physical damage. Mentally I was being tortured, and part of me believed the accident was retribution for the type of person I'd become. The way I treated people was a disgrace, my arrogance was second to none, and more importantly I'd never been an integral part of my wife and kids lives, always pushing them away and never showing my love for them. It came as no surprise when they eventually left me. In fact the most surprising part was that they'd hung around for as long.

I needed a drink to steady my nerves, but that was the poison that led to the current circumstances, so I dismissed the urge. I had to be strong, get my shit together and back into a normal existence again.

I headed for the bathroom, eager to see evidence of the successful surgery. Standing in front of the mirror, looking like an Egyptian Mummy, I started to slowly and carefully unravel the bandage. They said to keep them on for four or five days. Why give you the choice, like you're going to pick five if four was an option. However, in my case, four days wasn't an option either, I had to see for myself, see the damage I'd caused and what Alexander McKenzie had now become.

My pulse rushed like the gallop from a charging racehorse. It felt as though I'd just been informed that I had twenty four hours to live. I stared at the being in the mirror, tears again trickling down my nasty face. I just gasped, unable to utter a sound. Success my ass, I'd hate to see an operation that'd actually gone wrong.

I didn't know what to do or say. The inner pain had to stop, but I knew no other way than alcohol, but that wasn't an option right now as it was too much of a reminder of that night. I took myself into the bedroom and climbed into bed, pulling the covers over the top of my head and curling into a tight little ball like a scared animal. How the fuck could I face the world ever again? All the bastards staring at me and laughing behind my back, particularly those work folks. They would be the worst. I could just see them now, scheming behind my back, joking and giggling, then going all quiet as I entered the room, even though they'd be aware I'd just heard their antics. What about those who didn't know me? If I went to the Grocery store, would they treat me like I had the plague, or would they instantly look away if they came into eye contact with me? What about sex? Who the fuck wanted to bang or make-out with someone with half a face resembling a melted candle? Holy shit, I wasn't exactly piling up the notches on the bed-post as it was these days, unless jerking off counted. The only new piece of ass I was likely to nail would be if I decided to switch hands. I had to stop all this negativity, but the more I tried the worse it became. Going to sleep was the only option. Maybe that would at least momentarily numb the pain.

I tossed and turned for what seemed like hours, but my mind was still working overtime. I couldn't deal with this or with what I was going to have to face socially. The mental strain must've taken its toll on me, as I felt my eyelids becoming heavier and heavier.

We don't need your type around here. Take your twisted ass face outta here, this is the town of the beautiful people. Go on before we whip and beat you within an inch of your life, although it seems as though that might be doing you a favor, you ugly, evil looking bastard. Go on, get out, you're scaring the women and children. LOOK AT THEM, THEY'RE TERRIFIED!

"LEAVE ME ALONE, JUST FUCKING LEAVE ME ALONE" I screamed, awaking from the most horrific and barbaric nightmare I'd ever encountered.

This was a living nightmare though. You may dream of being stabbed or shot, wake up and grasp at the wound, only to realize it isn't actually there. You're not bleeding and it was all a load of fiction, but not in my case. I grabbed at my face, expecting a smooth feel or some stubble at worst, but it *was* real. The wound *was* there and the nightmare *was* real. I might not have been bleeding, but I was inside.

4

Back to Work

It'd been four weeks since I checked myself out of the hospital, and to describe myself as a social recluse would've been the understatement of the year. My only exposure to the outside world had been a trip to the grocery store. I timidly entered the overly bright shop, extremely self-conscious, even although I was clad in my hooded sweatshirt, which covered my melted face as much as it possibly could. I walked with my head down, leaning forward on the shopping cart, preventing anyone seeing my physical catastrophe. I was unsure how I'd react to someone giving me a horrified look. They were all still staring though, I could feel it in my bones, but I was fine with that. I did look a little suspicious walking around with a hood on and head down. Screw them though, they could come to whatever conclusions they wanted to. Hopefully they thought I was a burglar, rapist or even a murderer, anything other than seeing my face. As long as they were a little uneasy or even scared, because I was terrified, and needed to share the feeling.

Every time someone came anywhere close to me I almost had a panic attack. What if someone asked me a question like "can you tell me where the bread is"? I think I would've shit my pants. Maybe I should just drop the hood and hopefully they would run off.

I caught a glimpse of myself in the glass door of the frozen food section. The pain it caused was still acute, but I had to keep going. If this was payback for something it was certainly working. As much of an asshole as I'd been in my life, I'd never been one of those people who would've made fun behind a disfigured person's back. What the fuck was wrong with people who did? I'd never imagined the gut wrenching experience these people go through on a daily basis. The anxiety, pain and tears were probably a regular occurrence. I'd never let people treat the disfigured or disabled in a disrespectful way, even if the target wasn't myself. That had always been the case and I'd do whatever it took to prevent it.

I made my way to the checkout, the cart almost overflowing with groceries. I didn't plan on leaving the house for a while, so the cupboards and refrigerator had to be filled to the max. I exchanged a brief greeting with the cashier—head down of course. A line was beginning to form behind me, adding to the anxiety. It was taking forever, but the sheer volume of items made it unavoidable I suppose. It was a catch 22 situation, as less groceries would mean an unwanted return visit or two. However, more groceries avoided that, but increased the time in line, and in turn the number of people staring at my suspicious presence, probably wondering what I was hiding or indeed planning. Why the fuck couldn't they open another checkout? That would bring the heartbeat down a notch or twenty.

Finally it was over, as the cashier informed me of the total, which was roughly equivalent to the GDP of a small African nation. I didn't care though as I had to get out of there. I swiped my card, punched in my identification number and fled like a burglar from the scene of a crime.

The grocery visit had been over 3 weeks ago, but fortunately the fridge had a few items left over, although I was sure the cheese and remaining milk were probably hard to differentiate right now. I was right, but didn't need to smell the milk as a reference, as I could feel the chunks bounce off the sides of the carton as I gave it a shake. I cut up some of the cheese and put on two slices of toast before heading for a quick piss. I pottered around for a bit before finally making it to the bathroom—the relief was fantastic. I really should've gone a while ago, but I was a weird guy when it came to taking a leak. I would deliberately hold it as long as I could at times, as it made it all the more enjoyable when I finally went. It wasn't quite orgasmic, but it wasn't far off. That said more about my pathetic sex life than anything else, and with my new deformity, that was unlikely to pick-up anytime soon.

In mid-stream there was a sudden shriek from the fire alarm, which not only sent me into a moment of terror, but caused me to urinate straight onto my khaki pants, which is never an attractive look. FIRE, FIRE, FUCKING FIRE I screamed, running while still urinating, back into the kitchen. There was some smoke filling the air, but to my relief it was just the toast burning. The unexpectedness of the alarm though had caused all sorts of thoughts and memories to flood my mind.

I sat down in relief, letting my heartbeat calm down as I dried off the perspiration from my forehead. I began to laugh, as it was almost funny now. Shit, I was sweating like a gerbil in a gay nightclub as I sat there in my piss stained pants. There was a huge wet patch on the thigh, which to my amusement closely resembled the shape of South America. A trail of pee had also followed me to the kitchen, with its meandering, Amazon river like pattern being evidence of my unorganized and panic stricken attempt to put out the smoldering toast. It was good to have a laugh though, and I was sure if I could ride through the trauma that was now my life, the burning toast episode would make a great future story, assuming I found a friend I could share it with.

Today was the day for the return to work. I was sick to the stomach, but had to fight through it. I couldn't spend the rest of my days stowed away at home. My approach to fear had always been to look it straight in the eye. However, I was usually the one dishing out the advice, probably because I had an opinion on everything whether someone wanted to hear it or not. If you had a fear of heights, go to New York and visit the top of the Empire State building. If you didn't like doing presentations, do as many as you possibly could, as familiarity breeds confidence, and the fear becomes just another event rather than a traumatizing experience. It wasn't so simple this time though, as I was the one I had to give the advice to, and had never been on the receiving end before. I had to stay strong though and practice what I preached. I reluctantly left the house, continuously reiterating the advice in my head as I climbed into my car and headed for the office.

I sat in the car outside the office for about ten minutes, trying to build up enough courage. I so wanted my hooded sweatshirt, but it was hardly appropriate for a corporate environment. "Come on, let's just do this," I said aloud, climbing out of the car and heading for the main door. Fuck all of them, they didn't like me anyway, so what the hell. I was sure they already talked smack about me as it was, so what was the significance of another item to get their tongues wagging. That mental approach built me up a lot and I entered the office with a confident strut and shoulders held high. It was like one of those Western movie moments, when the cowboy enters the Saloon and everyone including the piano player stops what they're doing. Cheeseburger Eddie—as I disrespectfully used to call him—even stopped shoveling a huge breakfast sandwich into his chubby ball shaped face.

"Do any of you guys have a problem?" I said, just like something from the movie.

As soon as the words jumped my lips, their previous activities commenced again, just like I'd triggered a voice activated switch.

I was feeling good as I continued on into my office, but as soon as I closed the door behind me I collapsed into my leather chair. It was like a cocktail of emotions. On one hand I was nervous, as I knew I couldn't stay in here forever, but on the other hand I was on a high, as I'd expected something much different and less successful. The fact I'd left them feeling like the assholes made me almost proud, but this mood swiftly migrated to anger, as I could hear the muffled sound of conversation followed by an unwelcome chorus of laughter. Surely those fuckers weren't sniggering at me. What else would it be though? There was no doubt I'd always been a pain in the ass to work with, but business was business and I wasn't one for mixing it with friendship. However, I would never make fun of someone who'd just been though a traumatic experience or a disfiguring accident. Those useless pricks must really hate my guts. Well screw them all, nobody was going to make an ass out of me. I burst out of my office door, fully prepared to go on a complete rant about how they should be ashamed of themselves for making fun of the disfigured, and how they didn't even deserve feeding as a result of their cruelty. Much to my shock I was met head on by Paul and Jordan of our International Marketing team.

"Sorry about earlier Alexander, you just took us all a bit by surprise," said Jordan. He seemed genuine, but he was always a dick, so I was suspicious of his pleasantries.

"Yeah, sorry we all stood there almost lifeless, just hadn't realized you were coming back today. Hope you are doing OK and if there's anything you need, just let one of my staff or myself know. The face doesn't actually look too bad, sure it will be even better in a couple of weeks," said Paul.

I was left speechless for once in my office life.

"Sure, no problem," were the only words I could muster. I turned full-circle and headed back in sheer disbelief to the seclusion and safety of my lifeless office. What the fuck was happening here? They were never nice, any of them. I carefully thought through what they'd both said. As I analyzed their words, more laughter came from the outside office, and I could hear the faint sound of Paul and Jordan rallying the troops to further hilarity.

Then it hit me, they'd been full of shit. I was known as Alex, and Jordan always referred to me as Alexander when he was lying about something, although it was usually about the financial impact of a new customer contract. They were both lying little pricks. Everyone knew I was coming back today. It had probably been the hot topic of conversation all morning. I'd even go so far as them taking bets on how bad my injuries were. Like any type of accident that goes on in the world, there always seems to be a certain grace period before the jokes on the subject rear their inappropriate heads. Just as with the space shuttle disaster many years ago, it wasn't long before the acronym NASA was labeled 'Need Another Seven Astronauts'. They really hated me though, so I probably forfeited any minimum grievance period. As for their comforting gesture "to let them know if I needed anything, and the face doesn't look too bad." What a pile of crap. They wouldn't go out of their way for me if their life depended on it and I wouldn't even piss on them if they were on fire. Stevie Wonder and Ray Charles could've told me I looked like a monster, and at least they'd have the balls to tell me a couple of weeks wasn't going to do shit for me.

The laughter continued on and my patience was become thinner and thinner. I so wanted to know the truth. What were people saying about my face? This wasn't working for me and I couldn't take it for much longer. Maybe they would've been sympathetic to someone they liked or didn't know. They surely couldn't just be that cruel in general. I needed to know what people's consensus was, it was the only way I could work through this. Perhaps I believed it was worse than it really was, but I would never find those answers here, as they were already biased by the way I'd treated them all in the past. It was time for a change, and that change would begin this very minute. I packed up my belongings and headed for the door. It would be the last time I'd frequent this office building ever again.

5

The Messed Up Mind

My childhood began as a fairly normal one. I was never part of the 'in crowd' and not even that popular. I was the type of kid who just flew around under the radar, except for when it came to playing soccer—I was the best in the school. My Father was my hero, and had always encouraged me to excel in sports. He was a large man, with very defined and almost square looking features. He had jet black hair that always appeared to shine, except for the small patches of grey that were appearing around his temples. His job kept him extremely busy, but he *always* made time for me and supported every endeavor I put my mind and soul into—I loved him more than anything on the planet. He was my Superman and I always felt safe with him—until one horrifying and unforgettable day.

I returned home from school to my sobbing Mother waiting outside our house, car keys in one hand and paper tissue in the other. Her beautiful soft skin appeared to have aged since she cheerfully sent me on my way that morning, and her blood shot eyes couldn't have been further from the joyful vibes they usually emitted. She hugged me tighter than ever before, squeezing tighter and tighter as she told me of my Father's stroke. Why did the good guys always seem to be the ones affected by these types of events? Rapists and child molesters were healthily running rampant around the country, but my clean living Dad was dealt the unlucky card. Life just wasn't fair. I was motionless and void of any emotion—I wasn't completely sure what a stroke was, but from my Mother's behavior I knew it wasn't good.

Nothing could've prepared me for the moment I first saw him. My superhero seemed zapped of all his powers, but as always, tried to maintain an upbeat nature. He was still mentally strong, and was attempting to blow it off like it was a minor inconvenience, but I knew it was all a façade for my benefit.

He'd lost all feeling in the entire right side of his body, including his face. His speech was seriously affected, and at times I couldn't understand what he was saying, although I pretended that I did. I wanted to make him feel he was still fully comprehensible. He didn't need that added to his list of emotional worries. I'd never loved him more than at that moment. I wished I was older and stronger and could be his protector. It was killing me inside.

Time slowly became somewhat of a healer and life continued on. I spent every available minute with him, and even let soccer practice drop down my priority list, much to his disgust. He told me everything would be alright and that I needed to get back to focusing—which I reluctantly did.

The match was going well. The team was leading two to one, after I'd delivered a nicely timed goal just before half-time.

"Thuper goal kid," said my Father. His speech was still impaired, but I didn't give a shit. To my surprise, he'd dragged his ass all this way to see me play and I couldn't have been happier. The tears streamed down my face knowing he'd done this for me, and I'd never been so proud.

"OK enouth of the tearsth. Justh score anotha one for me."

I hugged him proudly as we made our way slowly to the dressing room in preparation for the second half. He dragged his leg as quickly as he could, attempting to keep pace, but it was too much for him.

"Go ahead thun, I'll catch up."

I listened to his every word and would never question him, so I trotted on, tears now replaced by a warm and fulfilling feeling as the goose-bumps covered my body like a rash.

"Look at this fucking retard," were the evil words from one of the opposition kids, as his fellow players erupted into hysterical laughter.

I turned to see my father as the target of their jibes. My happiness was swiftly replaced by a torrent of anger and rage. My body was shaking and I felt my blood boiling more and more with every chuckle. What happened next was almost a blur, but I found myself on top of the little nasty prick. I pounded and pounded on his head, and continued to do so even after his body went limp. I couldn't bring myself to stop. How dare he make fun of *my* Dad. Nobody would make fun of him or else they would pay. Not *my* Father, not my hero.

The wails from my Dad were too little too late. He'd tried to get there to stop the beating I was giving out, but in his hurried attempt he'd fallen over. I saw he was down and this only added to my fury.

That was the beginning of my concerning behavior. The kid on the receiving end spent a week in the hospital, but luckily for me there weren't any long terms brain injuries. His parents decided not to press charges, as a result of their son pulling through and in light of the reason for my actions. They said as long as I received counseling for my anger issues, they wouldn't take any further action.

It was a long and difficult process for me, but it did help significantly. It took a while to keep my emotions in check though. Anytime I was out in public with my Father I could see everyone looking and wondering. It made me so mad and I felt like killing them all. What were they thinking?

I became somewhat of a loner as years rolled by. Everyone knew I'd hospitalized that kid and always gave me a wide berth. I'd been tagged with the reputation of being a loose cannon who could explode at anytime, which wasn't too far from the truth. It was harsh though as deep down I was a good person who really meant well. I began distancing myself more and more from people, keeping my thoughts and actions to myself and developed a general dislike for everyone, becoming very arrogant and self-centered.

To this day I missed both my parents who'd now passed on. I just hoped all my gut wrenching and violent emotions were buried with them.

*   *   *   *

I knew I was still fucked up in the head, there was no denying it, but I looked upon it in a positive light. There was no pretending I was fine, because I wasn't. Life would never be the same again, that was for sure, but weeks and several therapy sessions since the accident hadn't cured shit. Screwed up in the head was the way it was going to be, but I had to get back out there and find out what people were really saying about me, I just had to know.

All this fake bullshit was driving me crazy. I couldn't really take out my frustrations on my old colleagues, they had every right to comment behind my back and I was fine with that. I'd always been a dick to them on a daily basis, so I was sure in a sick kind of way they didn't really feel too sorry for me. I had to make a fresh start, a new job and a new me. If I was a nice guy and the new work folks were making fun, then they *would* pay, that was a given. I had to think though, how could I find out what people were really saying? They'd hardly come straight out with it and tell me I looked like an alien. It would always be "it doesn't look too bad" type of bullshit response, even if deep down they were disgusted by it. It was becoming an obsession, but I was like a dog with a bone and couldn't let go.

For now though I was still an asshole, the only difference being I was a disfigured one. At least I'd save money on October 31st, no need for a costume when you looked like a character from Night of the Living Dead. Maybe I'd answer the door to the trick or treaters and let out a ghostly cry, while holding a flashlight to my face. That would scare the little fuckers. I was, and always had been a sadistic bastard, but it had a strange therapeutic effect on me. Some people would call it sick, but they could go and screw themselves.

It was like a revelation as the thought hit me like a ton of bricks. I could barely contain my excitement, and even let out a chuckle. Maybe I was losing my mind, but I'd discovered a way I could find out what people said about my disfigurement for real, but it was going to take a bit of time and a lot of discipline, not to mention a considerable amount of deception. Being the dick that I was though, the latter wouldn't pose too much of a problem. It would be the therapy I really needed. If people turned out to be nice, as well as sensitive to my trauma, I vowed to change the type of man I'd become. I needed to feel accepted, and not some type of leper if I was going to continue my existence. Why I hadn't thought of it before was beyond me, but better late than never. My preparation would commence immediately.

The Internet was a wonderful place, and I began my search. I was thrown a slight curve ball as I entered 'hand sign jobs' to the search engine and hit a masturbation link with the top match. I jerked off for about ten minutes to a young blonde sex-pot handling two muscle bound guys, with appendages resembling that of a large racehorse. She skillfully maneuvered like a champion cow milker, and it was like stereo as Muffin the Mule, Dobbin the Donkey and myself simultaneously groaned with satisfaction.

I quickly got back to the task in hand, so to speak. I had to stay focused, but fun for one was my only sexual outlet for now and would probably be the case for some time to come.

Eventually I found a fantastic website that gave a wonderful tutorial on sign language. It had an alphabetical home page, with the hand sign equivalent for thousands of words in the English language. I had no idea there were so many. The only sign I really knew for now was how to tell someone to go fuck themselves. This was really interesting though and I spent the next two weeks mastering my new found information.

My plan was coming together, so I needed to take the next steps to bring it to fruition. In essence the idea was a simple one, but pulling it off created a load more complex set of issues, but I would tackle those as they arose. I was going to apply for a new job, pretend I was deaf and would be able to be around new people, close enough to hear them talk about me while they believed I wasn't exposed to what they were saying. It was so simple it was genius. That way I would know what people's *real* feelings were. I'd be unknown to them and wouldn't have crossed them in any way to bias their opinions.

The idea came from something my cousin had told me years ago. She'd been a student studying foreign languages as her major. Her final year was spent teaching English in Argentina. By being immersed in the local culture and dialect, it only enhanced her current Spanish language skills. Her appearance though made her stand out like a penguin in the Sahara desert. Her mother and father were originally from Ireland, and her red hair and freckled skin were not exactly fitting with the typical dark hair and sallow skinned Latin American look. About a month before she left for Argentina, she had a breast enlargement. She was very happy with the outcome, but hadn't quite bargained on D's being quite so big. It had been a huge step up from before though, as she'd been as flat-chested as a five year old boy and was very self-conscious about it. The issue changed to being self-conscious about the big tits, which was rather ironic in itself, but she was a strange girl in her own eccentric way. When she got to Argentina she used to go to local coffee shops and order only using English. She knew she looked like a foreigner, but refrained from giving any indication she spoke the language. She would sit reading her book, or in this case pretending to do so, and would just soak up comments from other tables that were related to her appearance. They assumed, for whatever reason, that their words meant nothing to this little Irish looking girl, and would openly talk about her large breasts and what they'd like to do to them or indeed cover them with! She discovered that her pale skinned, red haired look was quite an attraction to the local men, and her huge tits were just the icing on the cake. One day as she was leaving one of the establishments, she heard a good looking young man comment on how he'd love to slip his penis into her cleavage. As she walked past the group of guys she said in Spanish "I'm sure you would, but I'm not sure your dick is large enough to handle them." They were left speechless, but needless to say she became quite a hit with the guys, and to my knowledge is still to this day dating the guy who made the comment. I never did find out if his dick was big enough to handle her breasts, but the fact they are still together probably speaks for itself.

The next few days were spent sending out job applications. In the cover letters, I clearly specified that I was deaf and had been involved in a burn accident, and that I was looking to change jobs for the reason of needing a fresh start with my life. I took a gamble with the references part, citing two fictional people, both of whom would be myself. I listed each as previous managers, and the phone numbers were my home number and cell-phone. I would just disguise the second voice as required, but it wasn't like I'd have to do any face to face talking if I actually got an interview. I just hoped they didn't ask for an address to get a written reference, but that was a chance I was willing to take, and I'd figure that part out if the situation arose.

The fact that I was deaf may even be advantageous for me. In today's work environment there is often a required quota of disabled and ethnic minority that has to be met, in an effort to show you're an equal opportunity employer.

The next week was spent in solitude, with a mixture of emotions running through my head, the only exposure to the outside world being a visit to the 24 hour grocery store. Why I hadn't thought of that the last time was beyond me, but probably attributable to my extremely fucked up state of mind at that point. It wasn't much better right now, but I had my plan and it was keeping me going. The grocery store was extremely uneventful for once, but then again not too many people frequent these places at 3 o'clock in the morning, other than alcoholics needing more liquor or single guys, who like myself, hated dealing with the bullshit of the crazy aisles, jam packed with bossy women, their annoying kids and the unenthusiastic husband, losing the will to live while pushing the cart, wishing he could close his eyes and open them again, only to find himself on the golf course or at the bar with his friends watching the football. I was in an out of the place in about 15 minutes, again clad in my trusty hooded sweater. I just piled cans of soup and ravioli into the cart, but resisted temptation to stock up at the liquor aisle. It had been a while since I'd had a drink, but the sheer thought of it caused a shiver to run down my spine.

Then it happened, like a bolt of fate fired directly into my mailbox. I almost cried with joy as I read the letter:

Dear Mr. McKenzie

It is with great pleasure that we at Power, Hutch & Miller invite you to interview on Tuesday September 11th 2006 at 9:00am for the position of Senior Finance Manager. We were very impressed with your level of experience and look forward to meeting with you. Please except our condolences regarding your recent accident. With regard to your hearing disability, we will provide an interpreter should that be required. We are an equal opportunity employer, and any handicap is absolutely a non-issue with regard to our selection process.

Please let us know if the above date and time is unsuitable and we can reschedule. Otherwise, we look forward to seeing you on Tuesday morning.

Regards

John Power
Senior Partner
Power, Hutch & Miller

Holy shit, an interview, I could hardly believe it. There was no time for complacency though as this was serious. I had to be ready, especially with the hand signing. The communication part was the important piece, but I did feel the whole equal opportunity employer line and the speed at which I received a reply was a good sign that if I knew my stuff, I almost had a shoe in the door already. I may have been an asshole, but the world of Finance was like second nature to me, and I was always the go to guy. I think that's where much of my smugness came from in the first place. I viewed myself as the know it all, and everyone else should just listen and do as I said.

I was nervous and excited at the same time. Meticulously I planned my interview strategy. If I was stuck with the signing at any point I would have my little notepad and pencil with me to give a short written reply. I would write down my specific questions for them on a sheet of paper ahead of time, deliberately loaded with technical Accountancy related words in an effort to knock their socks off. The more they talked, the easier it would be. These guys were busy men, so it would probably last an hour at the very most. I just needed to be sure I was the one controlling the clock. It was all coming together nicely. Just some final sign language revision and I'd be good to go. This might even be fun.

6

The Sting

It was the day of the interview and I was already sweating like a hooker at confession. I wasn't sure why, as I'd studied my ass off and treated it like a University final exam. Last night had been spent cramming in all the material I needed and rehearsing every minor detail in my head. I was prepared like never before, but this was essentially fraud, so I didn't want any screw-ups.

For some reason, my appearance didn't bother me too much this morning. They'd been informed of the situation, but I was a little anxious to study the initial looks on their faces, as that'd tell the whole story of their inner thoughts. I timidly entered the visitor reception area.

"Alexander," said the voice greeting me, as the attractive lady with unbelievably attractive breasts beside the guy hand signed something at me. I'd no idea what it was, but it must've been my name or something. I hadn't quite gone into that level of detail as far as learning how to say names, but fortunately I could actually hear! She was a little thing of beauty, but there was no way I would even attempt anything of a flirtatious nature under such circumstances. There was also the fact I looked like a melted bag of shit, but I could always fantasize.

I said the word yes as well as I could in a deaf sounding kind of tone and accompanied it with a thumbs up sign.

"Great to meet you Alexander, I'm John Power," he said very pleasantly as the sign artist carried on with her hand puppet show next to him.

This guy looked like a million dollars. The grey Armani suit matched his slick hair, and his tanned skin probably achieved from an overpriced exotic vacation. As we shook hands, it also became apparent he was no stranger to a manicure.

I can read lips very well, I signed to her. If I need you I will let you know, I added.

I'd been practicing that sentence all night, and by the thumbs up she returned to me, I assumed I'd done an excellent job. It almost caused me to smile, but I bit my lip and decided to save my personal congratulations until later, as there was still much work to be completed.

This was a nice place. The interview room was more like a living room setting, tastefully furnished and there was a very cozy feel about it. I sat down opposite John Power and Madeline the interpreter. I really had to focus, as her breasts were unbelievable. She must've known this also, as they were on display like a couple of prize-winning melons. They were either fake or she'd taken push up bras to a whole new level. They looked like a couple of little bald men doing a bad job of hiding out in her blouse.

I gathered my composure and off we went with the questions. It was the usual bullshit as most interviews are. Why do you want to work here? What are your strengths and weaknesses? What makes you a suitable candidate for this position? Blah, blah, blah. It was a walk in the park, as my preparation had essentially covered all of these aspects. I could tell Power was impressed. He was continuously nodding as Madeline and her mammaries translated my signs.

I glanced at the clock on the wall. Twenty minutes had passed already. I figured it was time to take more control. I asked Madeline if I could ask some questions of my own, and to no surprise Power was more than accommodating. I'm sure he was an extremely busy man, so I didn't believe he'd put too much time into preparing for this morning. He was probably glad to take questions from me as I think he was running a bit thin on his list.

I presented him with my pre-set list I'd prepared the night before, all neatly typed, with correct punctuation and not a spelling mistake to be found. Thought it would be a good example of my attention to detail, as well as showing I'd put in a lot of effort for this position. I had ten questions on the sheet and I knew he wouldn't have time to cover them all, but it would likely limit my participation for the remainder of the meeting.

"I see you've put a lot of time and effort into your preparation," he said, scanning over the page. "I'll try and give you at least a brief response to them all, but I have another interview in about 25 minutes or so."

Fuck, I hoped it wasn't for this position, but I was sure it was. Regardless, he was doing the talking now and I couldn't control the outcome of any other candidate. I'd just take whatever cards were dealt to me and hope I came up trumps.

Power waffled on for a while, hardly pausing for breath. I could tell he was in a rush, but at the same time he appeared concerned to at least answer my well-prepared questions. He blabbed on about mutual funds, stock prices and maximizing ROI (Return on Investment). I was losing the will to live, and wished he would just fuck off, after instructing Madeline to get the baldies out. Fantasy was a wonderful thing.

I appeared as interested as I could, nodding my head similarly to the way he had when I was answering his crappy questions. I figured copying his body language was a good way to go. From an unconscious level, this often made someone feel comfortable with another person, and I felt it was a good strategy.

"I hope that covers most of you concerns Alexander."

I had no idea if it had or not, but nodded enthusiastically and gave him a smile.

"Yes, thank you," I said in my deaf sounding tone.

We all stood up, exchanged a handshake and headed back to the lobby. I walked behind Madeline, sneaking a look at her equally wonderful ass. This girl really had it going on, and she knew it. I had no doubt in my mind she was aware I was checking her out, as her walk seemed to have changed from before, butt cheeks wiggling emphatically from side to side, making her ass look like it was chewing a toffee.

"Thanks again Alexander, we will be in touch in a few days with a decision."

"I look forward to it," I said, again in the put on attempt at talking.

As I left the building, I glanced over at the waiting area, and Power approached another gentleman, obviously his next candidate. A warm fuzzy feeling came over me—this guy had nothing. He looked like he'd been dragged through a hedge backwards, just before getting here. His hair was a mess and he was obviously unaware that an appliance by the name of an iron had been introduced to the world many years ago.

All I could do now was wait and see my fate, but my confidence hadn't been this high in a long time. Maybe things were finally starting to look up for Alexander McKenzie.

7

The Acceptance Letter

I was still glowing with pride at the success of my interview performance, and even if I didn't land the job, I was confident that if I had to go through the same exercise again, I'd do an equally proficient job. Several days had passed by, but nothing had came in the mail other than utility bills and countless unwanted credit card offers, promising 0% interest on purchases and balance transfers for another two years. I fucking hated those things. It was like a competition to see who could out sell the other. They were all a bunch of deceiving bastards. The only legitimate competition in my mind was to determine who could print the smallest, almost unreadable font, sneakily outlining all the constraints on the supposed fantastic offer. They would offer these great rates, usually if your credit score was above 840, which I think only applies to a Mr. Gates who runs a rather successful software company. The other part that baffled me was the free air miles, one for every dollar spent. Then if you get the magnifying glass out for a closer inspection, it usually states something like "only applicable on the last Tuesday of December, after the post has been delivered and the outside temperature exceeds 90 degrees." Super deal if you live in Miami and your mailman hasn't been out on the beer the night before celebrating his Christmas vacation. Otherwise you're fucked and the card benefits are about as useful as a chocolate fireguard.

It was around 3 o'clock, and like the daily ritual it had become, I jumped to attention at the sound of the mailbox lid closing. Today's load was still a mix of bills, credit card offers and useless leaflets for discount windows and doors, together with other stuff I could never afford. My usual procedure was to fold up all the leaflets, stuff them in the pre-paid reply envelope from the credit card company and drop it in the mail. I didn't want their shit, so they could have mine in return. However, today was different. Intermingled with the daily crap was an envelope with the Power, Hutch & Miller logo on the top left corner. One thing was for sure, it was either good news or bad, and I tentatively opened it like a nervous school boy checking out his SAT results.

Dear Mr. McKenzie

It is a great pleasure for us to offer you the position of Senior Finance Manager with our organization. We were very impressed with your interview and more than confident you will be an asset to our business going forward, and assist in providing us with sound strategic Financial improvements, guiding us to our goals of increasing market share and overall profitability.
We request a start date of Monday September 24th. I will personally meet you at 9:00am at our visitor lobby.
Again congratulations, and I look forward to seeing you again on Monday morning.
Please respond in writing, no later than Friday September 21st, informing us of your decision.

Sincerely

John Power
Senior Partner
Power, Hutch & Miller

It was a victory, one for one, no ties or losses. Absolutely unbelievable is what it was. I was like a kid in a candy store for the remainder of the day, putting aside all mental negativity, and immediately working on the acceptance letter. I was eager to get started and finally begin putting my plan into operation.

8

1st Day at the Office

I had a strange air of confidence about me today. I entered my new workplace like I was the owner. I just had to make sure I didn't accidentally let out a few spoken words by mistake, but I'd rehearsed this in my head for a while now and was confident I could maintain the charade. Like clockwork, John Power was there to greet me, immaculately well dressed again, but without the cute little puppeteer this time, which saved me the hassle of signing for one, but on the other hand it would've been nice to get a view of that outstanding cleavage again. It was a thing of beauty and had immediately qualified her for membership to my mental "spank bank."

Power escorted me to the office area, making sure I could see every move of his mouth, obviously in order for me to read his lips. If only he knew. It was almost comical as we headed along the corridor, me walking forward as he went backwards. Several people we passed gave me a strange look, but for once I was unsure if it was related to my face or whether they were puzzled by the unique way we were marching around.

My office was on the second floor, and the layout was similar to my previous place, but that was no real surprise. These days the open plan, cubicle style design seemed to be a common one, with the only difference at times being the walls on each little 'office'. Unfortunately for the workers here, the company must've been limited with their start-up budget or something, and had installed the four foot high ones as opposed to the six foot option. Employees generally hated the smaller size, as it was like an invasion of privacy. Usually the Internet is a fantastic outlet for quiet points during the day, or those times when you need to grab back some sanity from the crazy corporate environment. However, there is always an element of guilt as you double click on the Internet Explorer icon. Who's going to see me? Will I get into trouble for doing this on company time? Secrecy was the name of the game, but these two questions were far more common without the extra two feet of wall. You're exposed for all to see as well as the office gossiping and criticism that goes along with it. Not me though, I was the Senior Finance Manager, which entitled me to not only a door, but real walls and a ceiling as well, so I'd have the added luxury of undetected web surfing which there would be plenty of.

As we approached my new office, Power almost tripped over a garbage can as he reversed his way through the open plan area. I heard a few sniggers from the workers as he stumbled, but remarkably he remained upright, just like a gymnast regaining their balance after a less than perfect landing. He continued on undeterred, like it hadn't even happened. I almost turned to where the laughter had come from, but an emergency alarm instantly rang in my head. I couldn't be reacting to sudden noises or general sounds, I was supposed to be deaf for fuck sake. That would definitely be the hardest part of this con, but practice would make perfect.

I'd been scanning the office as we'd walked through, and was pleasantly surprised by their reactions, which were mostly nods and a few smiles. There wasn't a freaked out look to be found. Maybe people who didn't know me just didn't care about disfigurement or other unfortunate conditions, and accepted people for who they really were. Either that or Power and his two partners had drilled them on what to expect, and to provide me with a warm welcome. Whatever the reason was, it was fine with me for now as I was feeling calm and not worried about having a sudden panic attack.

My office was superb, decked out with a leather chair, mahogany looking furniture, and even a microwave. Power informed me I also had a $500 allocation to purchase any other furnishings I cared for such as pictures and lamps etc. I smiled and scribbled on my pad 'I'd better spend it before *I* tighten up the budgets,' and showed it to him. He started to giggle.

"You're a funny guy Alexander. I like your thinking though."

I gave him a wink and a quick thumbs up.

"I need to head off for a meeting, but I've left some instructions that will help you get on for a little while. If you have any problems go see Mary, one of our administrative assistants. She's in the first cubicle on the right as you go out your office door. Sorry I don't have more time, but I'll check in with you later."

"No problem," I said in my deaf sounding tone, together with another thumbs up. I didn't mind trying to talk, as long as it was only a couple of words. I felt a little guilty as I did the impression, but the feeling only lasted a few seconds.

I logged into my computer using the details Power had left for me, and pottered around on the Internet for fifteen minutes or so, looking at the upcoming football schedules before deciding I should actually do something relatively productive. I went into the Accounting system they used, which fortunately was the same system as I used before, although it was as common as Microsoft in the world of Finance. This place was really doing well for themselves. Their positive cash flow was more than a little healthy, which was encouraging from a job security perspective, not to mention annual bonus potential. There was very little else I could be getting on with for now, so I wandered over to the large glass windows of the office and looked out over the common working area. They were all like busy worker bees, scuttling around, conversing in what was obviously business talk by the serious looks on their faces, and taking calls from potential customers, no doubt in an effort to sign them up for life insurance plans or investment opportunities that would only add to the already substantial balance sheet. I caught the eye of two guys, probably in their late thirties. I exchanged a smile with them, but quickly their smiles turned to laughter and they muttered amongst themselves followed by more chuckling. What the fuck were they laughing at? I wanted to go out there and confront them, and find out what all the hilarity was about, but I'd just got here and perhaps my paranoia was just kicking in. I could feel a panic attack coming on as my hand instinctively touched my damaged face. They continued to stare and my heart rate accelerated like a sprinter down the home stretch. I quickly closed my blind and almost collapsed like a corpse into my leather chair. Maybe it was all in my mind, they were probably nice guys who were already joking about something, but what if they were laughing at me? Surely they weren't, I didn't even know them. There was cruelty in this world, but antics like that were at home in the schoolyard, not with a couple of professionals in a corporate environment. I managed to relax and finally convince myself that I was letting my fragile emotions get the better of me.

Ten minutes passed before my heartbeat was back to a steady pace. I composed myself and headed out towards where Mary was situated. I needed some stationary supplies and Power had told me Mary could hook me up with whatever I needed. To my utter horror, the two imbeciles from before were at Mary's cubicle. They were actually making fun of her as I could hear their taunts. They were talking in a retarded type of tone and delivering sexual references that would've violated any company's ethics and sexual harassment code. I could only see the back of her head, but she wasn't responding back at them, so I knew she needed my intervention.

"Are your other set of lips like the ones on your face?" asked the larger of the two assholes, as they giggled like a couple of eighth graders.

"They probably are Andrew. You should get a job down at the local circus rather than a place like this," responded the smaller asshole.

How could they? It was apparently obvious to me now that my earlier exchange with them was indeed about my disfigurement and not another paranoid episode as it so often was. So the big fucker was Andrew. The name was immediately etched in my brain as the rage charged through my system like a white water raft down a violent stretch of the river.

I continued advancing towards them and the little prick noticed my presence, giving Andrew the asshole a nudge in the side. Like a couple of cowards, they quickly scampered off in the direction of their offices, giving out a comment, but only after I had my back to them.

"They're like a couple of long lost twins," said the little guy in his high-pitched cackle. Like this slender prick had model features! He was a dorky looking man with thinning hair and a pointy nose. His large buddy Andrew wasn't much better. He was obviously no stranger to the local pie shop. He had the belly of a heavily pregnant woman, and his doughy face could've actually doubled as a pie if his head had been lined with an outer crust. If only they knew I could hear them, as I was certain they wouldn't have been quite so brave. I was in a state of shock as well as rage, but Mary quickly distracted me from the emotional rollercoaster. She was in tears and had a handkerchief covering most of her face. Why did they refer to us as long lost twins? As she dried her eyes and removed the paper tissue, all became clear.

Her mouth was disfigured, and by the looks of it, she'd suffered this stigma from an early age. It appeared to be a cleft pallet or something of that nature, usually a physical defect straight from birth. Her top lip was almost cut off in the middle and her speech was obviously impeded as a result.

"I'm solly about that," she said almost embarrassed. I knew she was saying sorry, but her hindrance obviously resulted in her letter R's being pronounced as L's.

"It's OK," I said in my deaf tone.

In her fluster, she'd forgotten that I was deaf, and this added to her embarrassment.

Other than her lip, she was an attractive woman. She dressed in a very old fashioned style, way beyond her years, but she appeared to have a nice body and her long brown hair was a delight. Her fashion sense probably only added to the torment she went through with those jerks, but she seemed to be in mental pain, and making herself glamorous was probably the least of her worries.

I scribbled on my pad that I needed some notebooks, post-it notes and a calculator. She smiled through her red cheeks and ushered me to follow her. As we walked to the stationary cabinet, I could see her nervously glance towards the other side of the office. I traced her glare, only to find Andrew and the other little prick watching us. I turned away, not wanting to give them additional fodder for their taunts. My blood was beginning to boil once again. It had calmed down to a simmer, but the mere look on their smug faces was enough to turn my internal stove up to maximum power once again.

"It's a retarded match made in heaven I think," said Andrew, oblivious to the fact I could hear every word of his animosity.

I could tell it affected Mary, as a hurtful cringe appeared on her furrowed brow. I carried on as best as I could, but the disappointment was chiseling away at my mind like a creative sculpture. I had such high hopes of being accepted in a new environment, but I'd just arrived here and was already being subjected to abuse from a couple of the sickest bastards I'd ever encountered. How long had Mary been putting herself through this torrent of cruelty?

Stationary in hand, Mary and myself headed back to her cubicle. She had such kind eyes and looked at me like nobody had for a long time. They were piercing blue in color, hindered slightly by the blood-shot red from her earlier tears. She didn't deserve the mistreatment and neither did I, but she was defenseless and an easy target for these mindless bastards. If only they knew I was aware of their antics. One thing was for certain, they were going to find out. I tried to hold back any violent thoughts, but it was becoming a losing battle. The kids when I was younger at least had age as an excuse for their behavior, but these guys were just plain evil.

I sat with Mary for the next hour as I had nothing better to do for now, at least until Power came back to my office. We talked for a while, as she exchanged words and I scribbled on my pad. She said that I might have some trouble reading *her* lips, which was a great line considering her condition, and we exchanged some laughter as a result of the witty remark. The laughing seemed to have a therapeutic affect on her, and changed her demeanor immediately. To me it was a sign that she didn't laugh very often, likely a result of the two bozos from earlier.

'Who were the two guys from before,' I wrote.

"Andlew and Chlis," she replied, and I could almost see her physically tremble at the mere mention of their names.

Andrew and Chris would be in for a huge surprise one of these days. If only they knew what was in store, perhaps they would let up with their mocking, but they didn't deserve the luxury of a reprieve in my opinion.

I'd finally found a friend, one who obviously accepted me for who I was, and could understand the mental anguish that disfigurement caused. It was like we'd known each other for years, as I explained to her about my accident and she told me of her years growing up with a cleft pallet. I found myself strangely attracted to her, and from her subtle body language I could feel she was drawn to me in a similarly bizarre way. I wanted to open up to her even more, tell her I could actually talk, but it was way too soon and I couldn't risk potentially freaking her out. I could help her and really wanted to. I could end the pain for her once and for all, but I had to be patient.

I glanced over to where Andrew and Chris were previously standing. To my dismay they were still there. Did these pricks ever do any work? They were stalking us like a Lion tracking down its prey. They were whispering something to each other, no doubt of a condescending nature. Again they went with their laughter. I may have been deaf, but blind I was certainly not. I glowered at them in a way that would've drilled a hole in reinforced concrete. It must've had evil written all over it, as their smugness turned to a look of fear. They knew I was onto them and they dispersed their separate ways. They needed to feel the pain. They were criminals in my mind and had a sentence coming to them like they wouldn't believe. The time wasn't right, but it was coming in due course. My initial plan had just taken a ninety degree turn, but I was excited by it in a sick sort of way. Pay back would be sweet. I didn't even know these guys, but that hadn't stopped them rubbing salt in *my* wounds.

9

Mary the Mouth

I hated the way they made fun of him, but I wasn't surprised by their cruelty, as I'd been exposed to it for over a year now. Alexander was a wonderful man, and my feelings for him over the three months he'd been with the company had been growing by the day. I felt safe around him and for once I had something to look forward to on a daily basis, which made me smile, an emotion I thought had been lost forever.

In a strange kind of way it comforted me that Andrew and Chris extended their wickedness to him, as I now wasn't alone to the ridicule. At least he couldn't hear their jokes and insults. I'd endured this all twenty nine years of my life. I figured that my middle and high school years would've been the worst, as kids in general can be cruel to those less fortunate than themselves, but I couldn't have been further from the truth. It hurt even more now, and every day was still like a punishment, the only difference now being the moments that Alexander was around me. My faith in God, which I'd once pursued as an avenue to ease the pain, had long been thrown out the window, and I no longer believed in a higher power. These adults I worked with were supposed to be educated and responsible individuals, but Andrew and Chris were just plainly evil imbeciles. Many of them kept themselves to themselves, and were in essence good people, but they would never stand up to the bullies who contributed to my daily hell.

I'd often thought about leaving and finding myself a new job, but I didn't think I could stand going through the same events at another place of employment. It was what it was and I knew it wasn't going to change.

At the end of the day I needed the money and decided to soak up the pain, keep my head down and get on with it the best I could. I hoped that one day I'd get to work and discover that the two ring leaders of the humiliation had be killed in a freak rock climbing accident or something. I knew it was wrong to sink down to their level, but death would be the best thing for them. If only they understood my heartache, my daily anxiety and panic attacks. Maybe they'd understand then, but that was just wishful thinking. They were the scum of the earth, the lowest of the low and needed to be brought down a peg or two. I'd considered approaching our Human Resources department, but it was like a big buddy system in this place. The bullies, Andrew and Chris, were senior level people themselves and played in a regular weekend foursome at the local golf course with their colleague Derek, who just happened to be the Human Resources Senior Manager. Taking them on would've been like walking blind into a minefield of red tape, corporate bullshit and ultimately further ridicule.

Living with a cleft palate was always a traumatic experience. I wished I'd undergone surgery of some sort, but growing up my parents were religious people who believed you were dealt your cards for a reason, and nature shouldn't be interfered with. They may have accepted and loved me for who I was, but why they didn't have the foresight to see that others were not of a similar mould to them was beyond me. I grew up used to the ridicule, even though it was torture, but accepted that my life was destined to be a miserable existence. It was still going along in line with that early premonition.

To Andrew and Chris I was known as Mary the Mouth, usually a term given to someone who talks a lot and not someone with a horrific birth defect. They often addressed me as Maly (pronounced May-Lay), due to the way my speech was impeded, which was an unavoidable result of my disfigurement. Other times they would just talk to one another in a retarded sounding accent, always when they knew I was within earshot. I wanted to scream at them, cry loudly and I'd even considered unexpectedly stabbing them in the eye with a pencil. Killing them both with a slow torturous death was not so much a recurring dream as it was a genuine fantasy, but I could never act on the violent thoughts. I was the type of person you'd take deer hunting and wouldn't be able to pull the trigger. I could go alone for the ride, load the guns, but never be the slayer. I couldn't even bring myself to express to them the ache they caused me. They thrived on weakness, and this would only add fuel to their fire of mockery.

Alexander didn't deserve this treatment. They only made fun of him because he couldn't hear. He was a big man, and they were way too cowardly to act that way if he was capable of hearing them. That was the difference. They made fun directly to my face, but as far as I was aware, only to him when his back was turned. I couldn't bring myself to tell him of their actions towards him. He'd been through a lot, and it would be easier for him not to know. It was enough that one of us was aware of their evil minds.

I wished I could spend more time with Alexander, even start a relationship with him. He made me feel good about myself, but I couldn't risk the potential rejection and end up losing the one good thing left in my pathetic life. I'd been celibate for over five years now, although it wasn't a voluntary decision. Who would want to be seen arm in arm with someone who looked like me? I was almost a social recluse, spending most of my time stowed away in my dreary one bedroom apartment, with nothing more than a vibrator and television to get me through the long nights. Maybe one day he would ask me out to dinner or something, then hold me in his strong arms or just whisk me away to somewhere far away from here, perhaps a quaint little country retreat, so we could start life again without the influence of nasty people like we were subjected to now. That was my wish, but it would probably remain as one, although I loved to dream about it, it made the long nights pass a lot faster and much more satisfying.

10

Hannibal Smith

I'd reached breaking point and couldn't take it anymore. These bastards were going to pay for their cruelty, not only towards me, but for the daily torture they put Mary through. She was such a sweet girl, and my feelings for her were getting stronger and stronger. She understood my pain, as I'd overheard her and her friend Monica, a fellow administrative assistant. She was telling her I was probably very self-conscious and suffered from anxiety just like her. She also thought I was "adorable", which was a description I thought I'd never hear again. She was just a beautiful person, and was the last human being on the planet who deserved such humiliation and disrespect.

"I'm so glad Alexandel doesn't heal the things they say about him. I suffer everyday, but nobody else needs that," I heard her tell Monica.

If only she knew. She would know, eventually I would tell her, but only when I felt the time was right. It was coming soon, but there were a few pieces of the puzzle missing for now, but I was getting close. I loved it when a plan came together. I smiled as I visualized the same words from the character Hannibal Smith in the A-team. He always had that little smirk as he uttered those words. Those evil fuckers Andrew and Chris were going to feel the pain and humiliation, but their pain would be more physical than mental, and I'd see to it they'd never be able to put anyone else through what Mary was having to deal with.

I had to move soon, as it was such a fine line between maintaining my cool, and just losing it right here in the office for all to see. I'd been hearing every word those fuckers had been saying behind my back. They had even named a sandwich after me, calling it the "McKenzie Melt", referencing my melted face, but you had to toast it a little too long so it was burned around the edges! How evil could these guys possibly be? I was a dick over the years, but never just plain monstrous.

Today was the final straw. There had even been a hand sketch on a sheet of A4 paper put on display in the gent's bathroom. It was labeled "Alexander & Maly's Lovechild." It was an abomination, but I was just glad Mary didn't have to see it. Looking at the drawing of the kid sent chills through my spine. Its face was completely burned, with skin hanging off it and the deformed lip was exaggerated beyond any possible extreme. I removed it from the wall, folded it a few times and slipped it into my back pocket. Maybe I would show this to Mary after all. I wanted her on board with my plan, and this might just be the deal clincher.

11

Partners in Crime

Tonight was the night to come clean. I left a note on Mary's desk, "Would you like to come for dinner with me tonight?"

I was positive she would be up for it. Even if she was unaware of my desire for her, she would probably appreciate some friendly company.

Sure enough, she came by my office with a warm smile beaming across her face like the rising sun. We arranged to meet at a local Italian restaurant after work. It was only an hour until we finished, but my nerves were kicking in and the time seemed to drag on for an eternity. I was not only nervous about confiding in her, but I hadn't been out with a woman in a while, so my confidence in that area was at an all time low.

Tonight was definitely the perfect night though. Prior to my invitation, Mary had seemed like she was in a daze, timid as a mouse and obviously avoiding human interaction as much as possible, as she'd been away from her desk much of the afternoon. She'd probably been through another barrage of insults from Laurel and Hardy and reached her mental breaking point. No doubt she had locked herself away in one of the bathroom stalls, free from the pain and comfortable in her own little world. Little did she know I was close to giving her a permanent get out of jail free card. I just hoped it would be appreciated, but it was unlikely to be otherwise. I was just as fucked up in the head, but mentally I was stronger. I had the ability to end the punishment. For her, entering those office doors every day must have felt like walking into an eight-hour torture chamber, so I was almost certain I could confide in her and share my secret, but more importantly my plan for both those torturing fuck heads.

I may have been wrong, but I was sure she was bursting to tell me of her pain. I think she trusted me, and the way she looked into my eyes had my pulse racing every time. Her lip in my opinion wasn't too badly out of shape, but in her head it was catastrophic. She'd obviously been through the entire escapade with Monica, but she couldn't help her.

I sat at the restaurant table waiting on her arrival. I could feel the array of eyes from the other tables, sneakily scanning over at me for a quick look at the freak show. My plan did not involve them though. Finally she appeared, grinning as he saw me, but there was sadness in her eyes. No doubt those pricks had given her a hard time before she left the office. She had really made an effort, putting on some make-up and lipstick, which was likely the target of their latest jibes. In my eyes she looked wonderful, so caring, loving, and had so much to give and live for. Her efforts to look good made it almost feel like a date, which revitalized my previously diminished confidence.

"Hi Alexandel," she said as the waiter courteously helped her get seated.

"Hi Mary," I said in my real voice. There was no time like the present to get this moving.

She was speechless, which was ironic in the current situation. Her mouth was open, but no words were coming out. You would've thought I'd suddenly asked if I could stick my cock in her ear.

"I'm sorry to throw this on you, but I'm not deaf. It's all been a lie, but I need to explain to you."

Her next look confused the hell out of me. I couldn't tell if she was still in shock or whether she was disappointed that yet another element of deceit and deception had touched her life. I had to move fast.

"I hear the way Andrew and Chris treat you Mary, I've known all along. I know the way they talk about my disfigurement as well. That was the reason I kept up the pretense of being deaf. I needed to know what people really said about my face. Nobody in my old job would come clean and I knew they were talking behind my back. I had to go somewhere that people didn't know me, find a way to hear what they really thought. It was the only way. I was going crazy in my mind and I had to know. It's all been a lie, but there was no other way, I had to do it. I just wanted to come clean with you because I respect and care for you deeply."

"I'm listening," she said. She was coming around and even seemed curious. I kept going, but almost lost my train of thought—the idea of sticking my cock in someone's ear strangely amused me.

"Mary, I've not always been a nice person. Before my accident I would never have won any popularity polls at work. I was a hard task master and not always respectful of other people's feelings. After the accident they were being nice to me. They were never nice to me. I wanted to end my life, look at me. The only way I had a chance preventing that was to really find out what people thought. It may seem stupid, but it was eating away at my brain. By coming to a new job I could gauge how people reacted. They wouldn't know me, so they wouldn't be biased like my previous colleagues. I had to be around them though to hear for myself. That's where the role of being deaf came into the equation. They could talk without thinking I could hear them. It was the perfect situation, but I'm heartbroken and angry. I want something bad to happen to Andrew and Chris. They are evil and vicious bastards who don't deserve the luxury of air."

I may have been a bit too passionate towards the end, but it felt good to get this out.

Tears began to fill Mary's eyes.

"I'm sorry Mary, I didn't mean to upset you. I know this must all be a bit confusing and surprising for you. The last thing I would ever want to do is upset you."

"I'm not upset Alexandel. I'm sulprised by all this, and didn't see it coming in a million yeals, but I feel the same towalds those guys, they'le killing me. Evely time I think about them it makes me cly, but thele's nothing I can do about it."

"There is Mary, and I want to help us both. We can talk about it here after we eat, assuming you still want to have dinner with me."

"Of coulse I want to have dinnel with you. I cale about you as well."

"Let's start over again, and really get to know each other."

"I like that idea."

We were getting on like a house on fire. It had gone a lot smoother than I'd anticipated. She must've really cared for me. I wanted to hold her in my arms and promise her everything would all be alright. We were in our own miniature world, oblivious to the stares from the other diners. We were an odd looking couple, there was no doubt about it, but in my mind it was fate. We were meant for each other and nothing was going to fuck that up for us, particularly Andrew and Chris.

"So is this just two friends having a meal or can I consider it a first date?"

My confidence had grown, much like the lump in my pants, and I had no problem asking her what this meeting really was.

"I thought it was just two fliends having dinnel, but I'd plefel if it was a filst date," she said, with a huge grin appearing on her face and an element of blushing raced onto her pretty dimpled cheeks. I felt like I'd won the lottery. I wanted to swipe all the plates and glasses from the table, including the table cloth, throw her down and have my wicked way with her right there and then. I was almost bursting from my pants now, like a newborn python piercing through its Mother's egg, and decided the plan for Andrew and Chris could really wait until after breakfast if necessary.

"You and me both, I've been eager to ask you out for a long time now, but I didn't want to risk the rejection. I think about you all the time Mary, during the day, after work, lying in bed at night."

"Lying in bed at night?" she said with an inquisitive look.

"Well.... you know.... I don't mean.... I think about you a lot is what I'm trying to say."

"That's a shame, I had my hopes built up thele for a minute."

"Well I have.... you know ... while thinking about you. Oh my God, I'm sorry, I didn't mean....". What a stumbling idiot I was. I went from confident Don Juan, world renowned lady killer, to the acne ridden teenage Trekkie fan who had as much contact with woman as he did with a tube of Oxy 10.

"I'm just messing with you Alexandel. If it's any consolation, I think about you when I'm lying in bed at night, and usually when I'm with my fliend."

"With your friend." I was completely confused, but I was being as attentive as a straight A student.

"Not that type of fliend. This type of fliend doesn't talk to me, but celtainly costs me a lot on battelies."

Championship! What a result. Maybe I should've seen it coming. I was ecstatic, and as delighted as a blind gay guy landing a job at a hot dog factory.

"Check please," I joked, simulating I was calling the waiter.

"That sounds like a good idea to me."

We took my car back to my place. The details of my plan would have to wait until later, but I had no issue with that, the complete opposite to be specific. On the ride home we didn't say too much. Maybe it was nerves, but we shared many provocative glances on the journey home. We were almost drooling over one another like a ravenous dog to a fillet mignon. I was convinced that had I been racing Dale Earnhardt Jr. back to my place I would have kicked his ass with room to spare. I was already undressing her in my mind, to such an extent that I ran a red light. Fortunately the road was quiet and no Police were around, and I don't even think Mary noticed the potential catastrophe as she rubbed around my knee and inner thigh. I had to speed up as any more of her tender touch was undoubtedly going to lead to an accident, not involving any cars, but definitely concerning the interior of my pants.

We finally made it to my driveway and we bolted out of the car and towards the front door like a SWAT team to a drug bust. Mary was very nimble on her feet, which was more than I could say for myself. I limped as quickly as possible behind her, being careful not to damage my swollen appendage.

It was everything I'd hoped for and more. We lay back, panting like greyhounds after a four lap race. The actual act itself hadn't taken too long, but five minutes was over twice as long as I'd first anticipated, so chalked it down as a moral victory considering I was very much out of practice. It was so much more than a quick screw though. I was really in love and knew it was mutual by the way she snuggled in close to my side, almost squeezing the wind out of me. We shared another kiss. It was certainly different to anything I'd experienced before, due to her lip deformity, but only in shape. They were still tender, and her bottom lip was just like any other. I nibbled and sucked on it gently, running my tongue over it in the process, which much have been doing it for her as she increased her already Anaconda like grip around me. I was struggling for air, but I didn't care. This was a magical moment beyond my wildest dreams. I had something to live for again. Maybe we should just run off together and forget about those two evil bastards, but I couldn't let it go. They had to suffer the pain they put us through, especially Mary. Otherwise they would just carry on to their next victim and begin their sordid process all over again. That wasn't going to happen.

We sat down to a hearty breakfast of bacon, eggs, sausage and hash browns. I needed the fuel as a result of our early morning marathon sex session that may even have woken the neighbors. I thought I made a lot of noise, but Mary was like a screaming banshee. It was so hot it made me want to go again, but my recovery skills apparently weren't what they used to be. We ate and gazed warmly at each other. We would never be displayed on the cover of Vogue magazine as America's finest looking couple, but the phase beauty is in the eye of the beholder was never more relevant.

As Mary wiped up the last of her egg yolk with her heavily buttered bread, I decided it was time to interrupt our new found harmony.

"If you had to pick two people in the world who could die today, who would you choose?"

"Is this a tlick question?" she replied. I could see her mood change as the horrific vision of the two stooges entered her mind.

"Kind of, but I'm going somewhere with this. I actually want them to die, not wish, want."

She was looking confused but intrigued.

"I do too, but you'le losing me a little."

"I don't want to work at Power, Hutch & Miller anymore. I want us to run off together and be happy. I know it's very sudden to be making these type of plans, but I think I feel better than I ever have when it's just you and me. But we need to end the torture these guys put people through. If we just get up and leave, they'll just move onto their next unlucky victim. You don't want that to happen either, would you?"

"Of coulse not, I wouldn't wish that on anybody. But what ale you suggesting?"

"I want to kill them."

"What?"

"I want to kill them. They deserve it Mary, they really do. I've played with this idea over and over in my head and I keep arriving at the same conclusion—they need to be put out of their misery."

"You leally ale being selious alen't you?"

"Yes I am. Mary, what they've been putting you through is criminal. Had they held you in a room and physically beaten you on a daily basis and were found out, they'd spend many years in prison. Is that type of torture really that different from the mental pain you've been putting up with all this time? I can't take their shit anymore. Look at this fucking picture. They drew this, I have no doubt. Alexander and Maly's love child. It's fucking barbaric."

My demeanor had changed as I stuck the drawing in her face. I could feel the vain on my temple pulsing in time with my increasing heartbeat. I was the conductor controlling this orchestra and I was mentally waving my stick in an overcharged frenzy.

I could tell she was in no doubt of my sincerity, but my last point must've hit home, and the initial absurdity of the whole idea changed to a pondering expression on her face as the initial furrow on her brow disappeared.

"We would nevel get away with that, would we?"

I was encouraged by her use of the word "we". She was actually starting to process this as an option, but she didn't have to, as I'd already ran the upcoming chain of events over in my head more than a hundred times.

"Yes we can. I've been doing a lot of thinking about this. I want us to be together in a place far away from here, and I want them to be gone forever. Would you really feel bad if their lives were ended?"

"Of coulse not, but I'd plefer if they were killed in an accident ol something. I don't want you ol I to get into any shit fol being involved. We've just found one anothel and I don't want it to end because of something stupid."

"OK, well we'll just pick up and leave, and say screw it to the next unfortunate person with a disability they set their eyes on."

"I don't want that eithel, but it's too much of a lisk."

"That's why our plan has to be flawless. We can do this."

I was really laying the word "we" down thickly. She was on the farmyard fence right now, but a gentle push would send her into my field of thought.

"What wele you thinking?"

Her balance on the fence was beginning to falter.

"I've been embezzling funds from Power, Hutch & Miller, diverting them into my bank account."

"You've been stealing! Pool Mistel Powel, he's such a nice guy."

"Yes, but we need the money to do this. I have plans for it that I'll explain later. The company has millions and millions, so a little bit here and there isn't going to hurt them. Anyway, with Andrew and Chris out the way, it'll be saving them money on two annual salaries, as long as they don't replace them."

I could be a real prick at times, but I'd found humor to be a great way to deal with anxiety.

"That's not funny Alexandel, this is some selious shit we'le talking about."

"I know honey, I'm sorry. I'm just trying to lighten things up, but I do know this is serious."

"What do we need the money fol?"

"I'll explain that later."

"No Alexandel, explain to me now. If you want me in on this I want to know what's going on."

That was a reasonable request, but I was going to keep one element a surprise. It was one present I was sure she'd be pleased about.

"OK, seems fair. I want us to get out of here afterwards, start fresh somewhere overseas. We'll need to leave work and it may take a while to get fixed up with something else, so we may need a good bit of money to do this, which is why I need to get it from Power, Hutch and Miller."

"Whele did you want to lun off to?"

"Rio."

"Blazil Lio."

"Exactly."

"Why Lio?"

"It's warm, exotic, and they can't extradite us from there should anything go wrong. Not that it will."

"Alexandel, I'm scaled."

"Don't worry about it sweetheart, I'll make sure you're protected. I won't let anything bad happen to you, trust me."

12

Identity Theft

My entire plan required a final component, and it was a major one at that. Not major like a dying favor from a long lost friend, it was *way* bigger than that. If we were talking about gorillas, we weren't referring to a muscular male Silverback, this was King fucking Kong.

I'd heard of Kieran O'Connell, but that was basically from newspaper stories linking him to organized crime, but nothing ever proved in a court of law. He was the local Al Capone, and not to be messed with. Screw him over and you'd be instantaneously fitted with a snug pair of concrete shoes and swiftly located to the land of the fishes.

One publicly known thing about O'Connell was his love of oysters, which he religiously devoured over lunch on a Friday at the Golden Diamond hotel's restaurant—renowned for serving the best seafood in town. That would be my opportunity to get hold of the final piece of the jigsaw.

I was shaking like a leaf as I made my way to the Golden Diamond. I wasn't sure how things would go down, but I was determined to make it happen. As I entered the hotel, I realized why it was classed as the most upscale hotel in town. The décor was lavish, sculpted marble floors with prestigious artwork and extravagant furnishings scattered throughout. I took several slow deep breaths as I approached the dining room and was greeted warmly by the hostess, even though the twitch on her lips was an indication she was wondering about my disfigured face.

"Table for one sir?"

"No thanks, I'm actually here to meet a friend, he's here already."

She gave me a nod and I made my way inside, scanning the room as I did so. I spotted O'Connell almost immediately. I'd never met him in person, but the large gentleman standing watch at the corner table was obviously a bodyguard. He was eyeing me intently as I made my way in his direction. O'Connell was oblivious, as he munched into his oysters like a starving prisoner, napkin tucked into his shirt collar as he slurped on his favorite delicacy. I was about twenty feet away, obviously too close in the mind of the bodyguard, as he immediately made his way towards me.

"Can I help you," said the henchman, in a tone indicating he was ready to kick some ass if necessary.

"I need to speak to Mr. O'Connell."

"Do you have an appointment?"

"No, but it's a matter of extreme urgency."

"I'm going to politely ask you to leave, no appointment, no meeting."

I glanced to the side of the oaf to check out O'Connell, which was no easy task, as he was built like a brick shit house. O'Connell had taken a break from slurping down his food and our eyes met.

"It's about my face Mr. O'Connell," I said, pointing to my right cheek, which was a little redundant as you could see the disfigurement from fifty yards away. This appeared to catch his attention, as his brow became instantly wrinkled. He summoned me to the table with a hand signal, much to the dismay of the meat head standing in my way. I wasn't home free just yet, as the muscle bound ape frisked me in a manner verging on sexual assault.

"Just need to make sure you're not wearing a wire or armed for that matter," said O'Connell in a very calm fashion. Obviously this was standard procedure and an exercise they'd gone through many times.

"I'll strip down naked if that'll convince you I'm not involved with the law."

I must've had a look of desperation on my face as he told me to "sit down" in a stern but inquisitive way.

"So who the hell are you? I'm sure I would remember that face if we'd met before," he said, much to the amusement of Hercules in the background.

O'Connell was not large in stature, but his reputation made up for any shortcomings in that area. He was younger than I'd imagined, and personal appearance was obviously important to him, very clean shaven and his short dark hair so perfectly formed, as though he'd just left the barber shop.

"We've never met, but I need a favor."

"A favor! Why the fuck should I do *you* a favor?"

"I wanna kill two guys."

This caused them both to erupt into laughter, but they quickly stopped. The look on my face meant business.

"Let me guess, you want me to get it done for you."

"Absolutely not, I want the satisfaction of doing it myself. They've caused me a lot of pain and they're going to get what's coming to them."

"So exactly where do I fit into your little master plan?"

"I need to hide my identity. I need you to put me in touch with a skilled plastic surgeon, one who doesn't ask any questions and isn't your normal above board type of guy. I need to be invisible to the law and I don't want to look like a fucking freak anymore either."

He slurped down another oyster as he pondered my little speech.

"Is that all?"

"No, I need two fake passports to get the fuck out of the country afterwards as well as a bank account set-up in Rio."

"I was being fucking sarcastic, that sounds like three favors if you ask me. You must want revenge really badly."

"I'm desperate and don't know where else to turn. I wouldn't even know where to begin to get these types of things, but these guys are going to die and I don't want to be recognized or even be in the United States after it's all over."

I intensely stared into his eyes, attempting to figure out his thoughts. It was like a game of poker as he returned the look, trying to read my mind. My desperation was real, and I hoped my eyes and facial expression portrayed it sufficiently.

"Do you have a cell phone?"

"Yes," I said, perplexed by his response.

"Put this number into you phone and erase it when the job's done."

He was certainly meticulous, obviously not risking putting anything down in writing, probably why he'd stayed out of prison for so long. I eagerly input the number, struggling to maintain my composure. This was going way better that I thought it would.

"When somebody answers, tell them 'I'm calling about the car you have for sale', he'll know then that you've spoken with me. From there all will go smoothly, expensive, but smoothly. We never had this conversation and I never want to see you again, now on your way."

"I understand Mr. O'Connell,"

I turned and made my way out, no handshake exchanged or offered.

"Good luck," voiced O'Connell, sounding genuinely sincere. Maybe deep down he could sense my pain.

I was shaking, but it subsided as I hit the sidewalk. O'Connell wasn't an intimidating looking guy, the opposite in fact, but there was a presence about him that *screamed* "don't fuck with me," that was impossible to ignore.

13

Face Lift

"I'm calling about the car you have for sale."

There was a slight uncomfortable pause before the gentleman with the husky voice replied. It appeared he wasn't expecting a call, but as O'Connell had said, all would go smooth.

"What time would you like to come over and see the vehicle?"

"As soon as possible, I'm looking to make a purchase immediately."

"Sounds good. Meet me at the following address at four o'clock this afternoon."

I nervously took down the details. It was finally happening and the reality of the situation started to hit home.

I headed over to the address around three thirty, giving myself plenty of time for any potential wrong turnings. I didn't want to be late, as these people were probably some serious underground gangsters and could perhaps be a little uneasy or suspicious of any delays. The directions were extremely precise, so I was there with fifteen minutes to spare. The guys were no doubt very detail oriented, so I wasn't surprised by the ease of finding the place.

It wasn't what I'd expected. The place was down by the docks and appeared to be nothing more than a deserted warehouse. I stepped out of the car, heart pumping as usual, which had become a common occurrence since all this activity had started. The place was deserted, nobody around and the wind created an eerie like quality, appropriate for any horror movie. I half expected some tumble weed to come charging past me as I approached the large iron double doors. I meticulously knocked five times, just like I'd been told to do. Any more or any less would've only led to potential suspicion and trouble that I wanted to avoid like the plague.

A small peephole type opening slid back and a large set of brown eyes stared at me with a steely look that could've caused a lesser man to shit his pants.

"I'm here to see about the car you have for sale," I said, trying to maintain my composure as best I could.

The peephole closed, closely followed by the sound of the huge door sliding open. It seemed to take forever before I was face to face with the owner of the beady brown eyes. He was a monster of a man, appearing void of any emotion.

"Follow me," he said in a complete monotone, not even any twitching acknowledgement of my skewed features.

He closed the door, and proceeded to walk across the open area of the warehouse. I followed like an obedient puppy, scanning the room intently. It was cold and damp, with the deadly silence occasionally interrupted by the sound of dripping water from a leaky pipe. There was a faint light barely visible in the far corner of the dreary open space. We quickly approached, and the sound of voices became louder and louder. We entered the room, which could've been a scene from any Sopranos show. The two gentlemen waiting there were neatly dressed with slicked back, but slightly puffy hair, and dripping with the finest of watches and gold sovereign rings.

"What the fuck have we got here?" said the elder of the two guys, addressing the other, but the question was obviously aimed at myself.

"Mr. O'Connell said I could get in touch with you."

I was shitting myself, and my voice was obviously shaking a little as the word "get" stuttered out in at least two syllables.

"We know. What the fuck happened to your face?"

I was starting to like these guys. A spade was a spade with these people. If they thought you were a prick, they would definitely tell you, no messing around. Not like those cowardly bastards Andrew and Chris.

"I was burned by two guys," I firmly stated.

I figured it was a lot easier to take that route than explain the whole mental torture thing. I knew it was a language these guys would understand, as I presumed violence and revenge played an integral part of their daily lives.

"Fuck one of their wives or something?"

Shit, they were really asking a lot of questions, but I decided not to object to that and continue with my convincing work of fiction.

"No, nothing like that. I was walking with my wife one night and we were attacked by the two guys I'm talking about. They knocked me unconscious and I awoke to find them beating and raping her. There was a funny smell of gasoline as I came around. It was on my face. As I tried to help her they set my face on fire."

"Fuck me," said the younger of the two gangsters. Even the beady eyed henchman had a look of shock on his previous poker face.

"What did the cops say?" said the top guy.

"Didn't go to the cops. I told the hospital it was an accident at home. I want fucking revenge on these pricks. To beat and rape my lady in front of me, then create this fucking monstrosity on my face. They don't deserve the comfort of a jail cell or wasted tax dollars on keeping them alive. They don't even deserve the fucking air they breathe."

I was even starting to convince myself of this story. It was certainly a more justifiable course of action, but mental torture had to be experienced to be understood.

They were really taken in by this rant I was going through, the younger guy shaking his head in agreement. Obviously he would've done the same in my shoes without thinking twice.

"I'd be happy to fuck them up for you, but it's gonna cost you," said the young thug.

"I'm not here for that. I'm gonna do the killing myself. I need to be the one who gives the payback."

"What do you need from us then?" said the main man, now sounding a little confused. They were obviously used to carrying out hits for people.

"I need help with my escape, someone to do plastic surgery on my wife and myself. I want to change my appearance in order to disguise myself, but also to improve this melted piece of shit. I also need two fake passports for us and a bank account set-up in Rio de Janeiro."

"We can take care of that for you. Gonna cost you a hundred G's though. No checks or shit, cash only," said the boss.

"No problem, whatever it takes. I'll need a couple of days to get the money together."

"We can do this whenever you'd like, so let's discuss the details now that we have a deal," said the young protégé.

"OK, I'll need the overseas account as soon as possible, and the name on the passport to match the account. Maybe need a week or so after I get the account set-up before the surgery."

The younger guy who I felt a strange mental connection with was keenly scribbling down my request.

"We'll get the passports ready, but it'll be about two weeks after the surgery before we can finish those up. I assume you want your new looks appearing on the photographs."

"Absolutely."

I actually hadn't given that any thought. It was such an easy detail to overlook as well. That's why these guys were the professionals and I was a mere amateur. This added a minor complication to the proceedings. We would either need to carry out the crime and hang around in hiding for a couple of weeks, or wait the same amount of time before committing the murder. The latter would probably be easier and safer. I wanted them to die as soon as possible, but I had to think of our future and couldn't risk putting that in jeopardy. Even with an altered appearance, I'd make sure they knew who was carrying out the torture before taking their one way trip to Hell.

"You still with us buddy," said the boss. I must've been momentarily lost in my thoughts.

"Yeah, sorry about that, just got a lot on my mind with this."

I'd become quite the skilled liar, a talent that could come in handy should any unwanted legal questioning ever arise.

"We understand. It's not too late to have us knock them off for you you know."

"Thanks, but I really need to do this one for myself."

"OK, call the same number in two days from now. Based on what you told us, say 'I'm calling about the gasoline'. From there we'll give you the bank details and schedule a date with the surgeon we know."

14

Under the Knife

We continued on at work as usual. Power was indeed a good man, and I was feeling guilt like never before as a result of his support and sincere respect he showed for me, but I had to maintain my tunnel vision and stick to the plan. Andrew and Chris maintained their antics full throttle, but I was soothed by the outcome that was approaching them. They really had no idea I was aware of the cruelty they laid on Mary and myself on a daily basis. Even Mary appeared to be less affected by their taunts and I was convinced she was becoming increasingly comforted by what was in store for them. She had no idea of the actual method I had in mind, and I couldn't bring myself to share the ferocity of my plan.

Things were going well, as I continued to funnel money into my local account that would ultimately pay for the surgery, passports, and off shore bank account. I was becoming a little rash with the deposits due to the time constraints I was working with, but I was the key financial controller and was tailoring the balance sheets to my requirements by editing each accounting line item to avoid any suspicion. It was an easy process, but one that couldn't go unseen for too much longer.

Two days had passed and it was time for the call.

"I'm calling about the gasoline."

"Do you have a pen and paper ready?" said the man on the other end of the phone. I was sure it was the younger of the two men from the damp and dull warehouse, but it was no time to inquire about who I was talking with. I excitedly took down the digits of the Brazilian account, my mind racing ahead to transferring more of Power's money to establish our future.

"Thanks for this. When can I schedule an appointment for the work I need done?"

"One week from today, same time and place as before."

"Perfect, thanks for your help with this."

"Let us know if any problems come up. If there are any complications, just call and let us know you don't need the gasoline anymore."

"There shouldn't be, but I'll let you know."

The phone instantly went dead. Now I had to tell Mary of the entire plan and hope she was still on board.

I'd made the call from the office, and was over the moon with the outcome. I was all ready to begin the money transfer to the Rio account, when I looked out of my office window to see the two pricks around a distraught Mary. It was like the starter pistol of the 100 meter race had sounded, as I bolted from my seat out to where they were obviously continuing the daily onslaught. They had their backs to me, but Mary saw me approaching. Her change in mood caught their attention, as they turned to see me striding confidently in their direction. Like a couple of cowardly animals they retreated back to their desks, but I clearly heard their "melted face mother fucker" comment as plain as a wolf cry on a clear winter night. Keep talking boys, you'll see what it's like to be me in good time. Now that Mary was aware of my ability to hear, her reaction to their comment was more evident than ever before, but I was unfazed right now and waved her to follow me to my office.

Behind my closed door, I asked her to take a seat as I closed the blind. I'd come too far to risk being seen talking to another member of staff.

"We need to be out of here in a week from now."

"What do you mean out of hele."

"I mean finished, not working here any more."

"Should I tell them I'm quitting?"

"Absolutely not, call in sick or something, but let's keep our options open incase anything changes."

"What ale you going to do?"

"I'll do the same. There won't be any problems for a week or so if we are both sick."

"Alexandel I'm scaled. I'm leally scaled."

"It'll be OK sweetheart. I'll make sure of it. Now I need to tell you something that I didn't tell you before."

She looked more frightened than ever before. It was as though she sensed something of severe magnitude was fast approaching.

"We're both scheduled for surgery a week from today."

"Sulgely, what do you mean sulgely."

She was clearly baffled by my comment, so I needed to explain quickly, as I could almost feel her pulse rocket out of control.

"We're scheduled for a face lift, plastic surgery to be precise. We need to disguise our appearance for what we have planned. I know it's a major thing, but we may look normal again and they'll have no way of identifying us after we get rid of these guys."

Her deformed mouth was open and she was trying to get words to come out, but she was frozen with silence.

"I know these are drastic measures, but I want a new beginning, one where we'll not only feel relieved, but perhaps look normal as well."

I could see her mentally digesting the thought, and her reaction was a positive one, much to my surprise.

"Look nolmal?"

"I'm not sure how normal, but your lip will be more like a proper one and my fucked up face should resemble something human like, as opposed to the mutant I look like right now."

"I love you just as you ale."

"I know honey, and I love you as you are right now as well. But this will hold us in good stead for the future. We won't be exposed to the ridicule that we take today and we will be out of sight as far as being tracked down should we be discovered. Think about it, no more mental pain and we'll be home free to live normal lives."

She was with me, I could tell from her expression. Her tainted, yet beautiful face couldn't hide her obvious excitement. I at least had led a natural existence before, she had not, so there was a clear appeal whatever slant you put on it.

"I tlust you Alexandel, so whatevel you do I am with you."

"I won't let you down darling."

We continued on with our daily activities, but I had to work fast. I figured the transfer of five hundred thousand would be enough. Shit, if Nick Leeson could screw Barings Bank over for hundreds of millions of dollars, I figured a mere half million was a drop in the ocean. Mary seemed to have a skip to her step for the rest of the day. It was obviously at the thought of having a regular appearance for the first time in her life. That only motivated me to get things moving even quicker.

Seven days were approaching fast, but the final two seemed to drag like back to back Monday mornings. My delight was reaching overdrive, but at the same time was nervous at the prospect of going under the knife. I had one final deposit of fifty thousand to make, but that was a sheer formality. The ridicule continued for us both, but it was as though we were now both deaf, Mary seemingly oblivious to Andrew and Chris. I could see them surrounding her at times, but she would look at me through my office glass with a smirk on her deformed little mouth, like an exhausted marathon runner knowing the finish line was now in sight.

15

The Surgeons

The wrought iron doors parted as before, and the beady eyed henchman again led us through the damp and dull warehouse. It was like déjà vu, but this time there was an air of excitement that almost nullified the sound of drips from the leaky pipes. We were led into the same office as before and welcomed with open arms by the younger of the two gangsters. He looked over Mary with a sympathetic eye, no doubt casting his mind back to the fictional rape and beating I expertly portrayed during our first acquaintance. She was well versed in my original story, but the details were never approached again. The transformation of the office was astounding and now resembled the interior of a surgical room of any local hospital. Two men appeared from nowhere dressed in their scrubs, and looked like any normal doctors you would come across in a medical environment.

"It's money time," said the young Tony Soprano type, eagerly rubbing his hands together like a new car salesman who'd just clinched his first ever deal.

I handed him a package, which contained precisely one hundred thousand dollars of Power, Hutch and Miller's money. His smile magnified upon inspection of the bundles of notes, unlike my bank manager from earlier in the day as I closed the account and removed all my funds.

"It's all there, count it if you like."

"I trust you, but I'll count it while you're asleep. You won't be going anywhere for a while."

That was true, but he knew I wasn't going to fuck around with him, and I was aware his comment about trusting me was based around this principle.

"Two weeks from today call our number again and ask for a follow-up consultation. Come back and we'll take your passports photographs. I'd also recommend you both change your hair coloring and even style. It'll only add to any escape plans you may have."

This guy left no stone unturned, and it was a great feeling to know my plan was only being enhanced as a result.

The doctors didn't utter a word and had their hygienic face masks on from the start. They obviously wanted their identities concealed also, and I could understand that.

"The doctors here have been working with us for a long time now and are extremely skilled in what they do, so stay relaxed, they will have you looking like a million dollars in a few hours. Well you will after the bandages come off in a week or so."

He was so calm in his delivery that I surprisingly felt at ease. I could feel Mary believing the same, as her vice like grip on my hand had loosened considerably since we first entered the warehouse.

We both stripped down to our underwear and put on a gown. It was just like a standard surgical procedure. We lay down next to one another on separate tables as the doctors prepared the anesthetic.

"I love you Mary."

"I love you to Alexandel."

The room began to spin and I felt myself quickly falling into a state of unconsciousness.

I awoke sluggishly, feeling like I was in the middle of a terrorist interrogation as I stared into the beaming light from the ceiling. Mary, or what appeared to be Mary, was looking intently at me through her heavily bandaged face. My hands instantly reached for my face and I felt the soft padding around mine also. We were like a couple of Egyptian Mummies, embalmed and ready for the tomb. The doctors were nowhere to be seen, and from their initial anonymous state, were no doubt long gone from the location.

"Told you you were in good hands," said my new found gangster friend.

"I feel like I've been run over by a fucking truck," I said, meaning every word of it.

"You've been through some major surgery, so I'm not surprised. Give it a few days and you'll be feeling like a new couple again. Keep the bandages on for at least five days. I do mean *at least*. There will be temptation to look, which I fully understand, but leave them be. The best things come to those who wait."

I loved his final line, which caused me a rye smile. I'm sure it was true in most cases, but Andrew and Chris were unknowingly waiting, although there would be zero best things happening in their very short future.

16

The Big Reveal

My mind had been cast back all over again to my original burn incident. This time however, the face bandages had been a result of personal choice. Mary and myself struggled to adhere to the five day requirement, but somehow with each other's support, managed to stick to the tough schedule. It was rougher for Mary though, as it was apparent something had changed. She no longer had her speech impediment. Regardless of her physical appearance, one significantly positive outcome had already been achieved that had her on cloud nine, and even more eager to look at her new face.

It was the end of day five and we both had the timing down to the precise seconds. We walked through to the same bathroom mirror that had revealed my original injuries. I was on tender hooks as I sat on my ruffled comforter next to the adjacent on-suite toilet. Mary was looking directly into the mirror and all I could see was the side of her heavily bandaged head. She began unraveling the cloth, slowly and deliberately, but there was an unseen sense of urgency to it. It only lasted a few seconds, but I could almost feel my hair growing during the process. The suspense was interrupted by her wailing sobs. I couldn't see her face, but the crying only increased in intensity.
"What's wrong sweetheart?"
My anxiety reached levels never before encountered, but she did not answer. She began turning towards me at a snail's pace, eventually finding my gaze as I peered back at her through the holes in my bandages. I could only then join in with her weeping.
The tears were those of joy. She looked beautiful, and she knew it. Some healing was still required, but her cleft pallet was gone like a long lost treasure, replaced by a full set of lips that could've filled in for Angelina Jolie in a close up scene. Her cheek bones were now elevated, and together with her knew lips, the name Mary the Mouth had taken on a whole new positive implication. The

crying continued as we hugged tightly, and although I was delighted with the unbelievable transformation, I was eager for her to let go so I could discover whether my surgery had resulted in an equally satisfying outcome. As her hold on me released I slipped through to the mirror and began the unraveling.

Holy shit, it was the old me again. Some minor scarring remained, but in essence I was the Alexander McKenzie from before. It was a sad day when the surgeons working for a black market organization were far superior to those working in the law abiding medical field. In my mind it was all about the money. Our entire health care system was so fucked up and ass backwards, pretending to give a shit and provide the highest level of care—they were the criminals in my opinion.

The emotion was on overload and tears continued to flow like water from an open faucet. Our embracing continued, but this time I didn't want to let go—I never wanted to let go ever again.

17

The Distinguished Gentleman

We spent the next week in sheer ecstasy. Our love making reached new levels of intensity, and kissing, which had been area of extreme self consciousness for Mary, was now replaced with the appetite of a starving tiger.

Mary had called in sick to the office, as did I. However, I'd informed Power that I had to attend to a matter of family urgency, but would work remotely in order to make sure everything was in check. I had to be sure all the books were in order and no financial red flags could be raised. Now was not the time to slip from the tightrope of success.

"I'm calling to make a follow-up appointment."

"We can fit you in at five o'clock this afternoon."

"Great, see you then."

The final piece of the escape plan was almost in place. We'd pick-up the fake passports and it would only be the slaying of Andrew and Chris that remained.

I'd been letting my facial hair grow over the past week and was beginning to resemble a rugged mountain man, totally opposite to that of my clean cut corporate image. It was all part of the plan though. I'd even bought some grey hair dye, in my efforts to further skew my previously deformed appearance. Mary booked herself into the local salon and was planning on transforming herself into a blonde beauty. She was on cloud nine and I was convinced she'd never been happier.

I dropped her at the hairdresser's and headed back to the house to work on my final hair trimming and new dyed look. I skillfully carved out a smart looking goatee, and proceeded to give myself a number three buzz cut all over my head. I applied the grey dye to the beard and head and waited a while before I could rinse.

I sat on the bed and contemplated. Maybe we should just run off without committing any felony, it would certainly be easier. But as I reflected, the image of those bastards infected my mind like an unwanted virus, and my blood began to boil just like before. They were evil, self-centered men, with complete disregard to other people's feelings. If we just left, it was just a matter of time before some other innocent victim was set about by these wild dogs. Nobody should have to live their lives in fear and ridicule. The decision was final.

I rinsed myself off and stared at my new look. It added years to me, but there was a distinguished quality that was difficult to dislike. I was almost unrecognizable from before and was convinced that if I showed up at work and entered my office, I would be quickly removed by security.

It was time to pick the stunning Mary up from the salon. I locked my house door for the final time and headed on my way. Tonight would be the big night for Andrew and Chris, and we couldn't risk heading back to my place incase anything should go wrong. There was no time to sell the place either, but that was OK. Power, Hutch and Miller had set us up with enough money to keep us going for a long time. As I drove I hoped the two arrogant pricks were enjoying their day, as it was going to be their final one on this twisted planet.

I pulled up to the salon around four o'clock. A smart looking blonde lady was standing outside, looking very pleased with herself—it was my Mary. I didn't think she could look any better than earlier, but I was so in awe that I almost mounted the sidewalk. Her hair was Marilyn Monroe blonde in color, but expertly cut into a symmetrical bobbed look. It was exquisite, and I had the urge to make wild passionate love to her right there and then. I needed to stay focused though, and there would be plenty of time for that.

"Oh my God sweetheart, you look like a million dollars."

"Shame I can't say the same you old looking bastard. I might need to find myself a new man who can match up to my standards," she said, giggling with almost school girl delight.

"Come here you sexy little bitch."

We shared a long passionate embrace before heading off for our passport photographs.

Again we were greeted by the monotone lifeless henchman, but even he couldn't maintain his emotions as he looked us over.

"You the same two from before?" he said with a puzzled look.

"The very same folks," I said smugly.

"Impressive, fucking impressive. Follow me."

It was the first time in our three encounters that he'd strung more than three words together. I was overjoyed by the fact he hadn't recognized us. That could only hold us in good stead for the future.

It was the same dreary place as before, but this time it felt peaceful. The dripping pipes seemed to add an element of tranquility, but it was obviously a by product of my new found piece of mind.

"Well fuck me," said the young mobster as we entered the office.

"Nice to see you as well," I said with a smile.

"Wow. Don't think I could put it any other way. If I didn't recognize your voice I would definitely walk past you in the street."

"That's what I'm hoping for."

"OK, let's get these photographs taken and fix you up with the passports. Then you can get on with your other business," he said with a wink and a smile. It seemed like he was looking forward to me disposing of the boys.

They had a pristine white screen already in place and a camera fitted to a tripod only a few feet away. Within minutes our shots were taken, and we eagerly waited to inspect the final product. We sat around in silence as the guys expertly went about their work.

"OK, two of the finest fake passports you'll ever find. Take a look for your-selves."

He wasn't kidding, they were incredible. I had a passport of my own and this was almost a clone with the exception of the picture.

"Absolutely fantastic," I said, barely able to contain my excitement. He could tell the job had been one of top quality.

"I believe that concludes our business," he said rubbing his hands together.

"It certainly does. I can't thank you enough."

"You already gave us one hundred thousands thanks, which is more than enough."

"I know, but you really don't understand what this means to us."

"I think I do. Now good luck to you and I hope we never meet again."

"We won't, you can trust me on that one."

We both left without giving the guys a final glance. He may have been a hardened criminal, but I genuinely liked the guy and knew he was sincere as far as understanding our gratitude.

18

Mattress and Matchsticks

An evening spent at the bar was a common ritual for Andrew and Chris. I'd made sure I'd researched their habits prior to this evening's events. I was positive these assholes were even more obnoxious with a gut full of alcohol. The one positive for them was that the beer would likely dull the pain that was coming to them. I really loathed both of them beyond the hatred of any historic rivalry.

I smiled in a smug yet satisfied sort of way as we pulled up in the alley beside the bar. Some may have labeled my mood as sick, but I would've disagreed. These fuckers deserved everything that was coming to them. My philosophy may not have stood up in a court of law, but their antics over the years had probably mentally tormented more individuals than Mary and I. In my mind it was equally as bad as physical torture. Had they dished out the physical equivalent, they would've been put in jail years ago, and the taxpayer didn't need the burden of paying for the upkeep of these evil bastards. Tonight I would be the judge and jury, and deliver a punishment appropriate for their crimes. In the eyes of some this was wrong, but in my mind I was right. Mary was behind me, even although I knew she was terrified. She did want them to die though, and had helped me with the final preparation earlier in the evening. We knew the light at the end of the tunnel was only a few tricky turns away.

"Wait here sweetheart. I'll give you a quick call when I'm ready for you."

"Be careful Alexander."

"Always."

I strutted confidently into the pub, and as I'd thought, the two disgusting pricks were seated at the bar laughing and giggling, probably at someone's expense. The bar was horseshoe in shape, and I took a stool directly opposite to where they were sitting. I caught Andrew's eye and he gave me a brief once over before continuing his childish chuckling with his equally insufferable buddy. I thought for a moment he'd recognized me, but that would've been impossible.

Perhaps there was a familiarity in my eyes that he connected with, but he appeared to be loaded and would never have expected anything out of the ordinary. I could hear the sounds coming out of their mouths, but was just far enough away to be unable to decipher the actual words themselves. Chris was doing what was obviously an impersonation of a retarded person, sticking his tongue down under his bottom lip and he blurted out some strange sounding noises. I glowered in their direction as I ordered a beer. Maybe he was talking about Mary, but maybe not. Either way my agitation was already on the rise and I hadn't even taken a sip yet. I couldn't even stand being in the same room as them.

Time was ticking on, and these pricks were really putting them back. This was a good thing, as their bearings and reflexes would be seriously compromised, but I was eager to get this show on the road. I had to maintain my patience though. The bar was beginning to clear out rather quickly, which was also working in my favor, as I didn't need any unwanted attention to interfere. I wasn't clear about how things would proceed, but Mary and I had discussed several possible scenarios, so it all depended on the surroundings and making sure we grasped whatever opportunity was presented to us.

"One more round barman and we'll take the check," said Chris, shouting over to the bar tender, much to my approval.

I quickly scanned the room after ordering a whisky shot. I needed to keep my wits about me, but the pressure was mounting and a swift glass of Dutch courage was definitely in order.

Including the bar tender, the dead men and myself, there were a total of seven people remaining. A loving couple sat only a stool away from me, but were a little worse for wear and more concerned with how far they could stick their tongues down each other's throats. The other gentleman was in his mid to late sixties and was staring into oblivion like it was his last day on earth. Maybe it was, so that would make three of them.

The boys chugged down their beers in super quick fashion and settled up their bill. Andrew headed in the direction of the bathroom, obviously to empty about ten gallons from his bursting bladder. He returned way quicker than I expected and they began to head towards the door. I slammed my shot and swiftly dialed Mary.

"We're on," I said to her as I followed the two fuck heads into the street.

"OK baby, I love you," she said, panic very evident in her voice.

"Now sweetheart, now."

"STOP IT YOU JERK, LEAVE ME ALONE," was the cry from the alleyway.

Even in their drunken state, the boys stopped in their tracks as they passed by the alley. Maybe they weren't as cowardly as I'd first thought, as they headed down the dark passageway in the direction of the distress call. I was sure they were a couple of pussies though, and their apparent bravery was just a result of the alcohol consumption.

It was all stations go as I made my sudden maneuver. I crashed my cell phone into the side of Chris' head and he dropped like a sack of potatoes to the littered concrete. Andrew was caught totally unaware and was too late to react as I grabbed him around the neck and slammed a chloroform soaked rag into his face. His struggling was brief as I felt his legs crash from under him and he lay lifeless next to the groaning Chris. I pushed the rag into Chris' nose and mouth and within seconds he was motionless also. Mary opened the trunk of the car as I tied their hands and feet up tightly with my rope and gagged their mouths. We carelessly threw Chris into the awaiting trunk and then worked on Andrew. Fuck he was heavy, most of which was located in his keg of a stomach, not really a surprise from what I'd seen from his earlier consumption. There was no time to become complacent, the fun was just beginning. We jumped into the car, hearts pounding like an epileptic drummer, and sped off in the direction of the rural forest.

The dirt road through the forest was a bumpy ride, one pot hole after another. The guys were still unconscious, as there was no sound of any struggling whatsoever. We passed the final set of large oak trees and stopped beside the fenced area of the open field. It was pitch black, and I'd already killed the headlights as another precautionary measure. We'd made the drive earlier as part of our preparation, so navigation was difficult but by no means impossible. I opened the gate to the field and we drove in, stopping just short of the open grave we had dug earlier in the evening. I carefully opened the trunk. The boys were huddled up together like a couple of newborn kittens.

"Andrew first sweetheart."

We had at least recuperated a little from putting them in there in the first place, but it was best to get the big guy over and done with first, he was the only one who could give us potential problems.

We wearily got to the graveside. I cut the rope from his ankles and wrists, removed the gag, and we rolled him into the grave. He hit the gasoline soaked mattress at the base with an almighty thud and we watched over him as best we could, but even the finest of vision couldn't have seen the bottom of the six foot hole. I grabbed the flashlight from the car and pointed it to the foot of the grave. There was a whimper from the beer gut prick, likely a combination of the fall as well as coming around from the chloroform. We continued to say nothing, but I kept the spotlight directly on his face.

"What the fuck," was his first words. It was my cue to talk.

"Not such a smart mother fucker now, are you."

"Where am I? Who the fuck are you?" he sniveled.

"It's Alexander and Mary from the office you obnoxious asshole. You're about to feel what it's like to be in pain."

"It can't be Alexander, that guy is completely deaf."

"You thought he was you piece of shit, but I never was. It was all a con to see what people said about my burned up face."

His panic was increasing as he realized he was under the ground and it became clear he was a little claustrophobic.

"LET ME THE FUCK OUTTA HERE YOU EVIL BASTARDS."

He attempted to climb out, but I stomped on his fingers as hard as possible and he collapsed like a dribbling wreck to the bottom of the pit.

"You're going nowhere pal. You're about to head to the land of Satan."

"WHAT'S THAT SMELL YOU DISFIGURED FUCK."

"Disfigured fuck! Still you persist with the taunting. The fucking smell is gasoline. You're going to discover what my pain was like, only you're going to have the advantage of not having to live with it."

"LET ME OUTTA HERE."

His cries echoed as I struck the match and threw it into the hole. Mary covered her ears and sobbed, as the flames crackled profusely. Andrew's screams were only short lived. Mary was a gibbering wreck, but there was no going back now.

I opened the trunk to a struggling Chris, his shouting muffled by the gag on his mouth. Mary was in no state to assist with this one, but that wasn't a problem. I pulled him out and onto the muddy field. He continued to squirm, but two punches in quick succession were enough to make him limp again. I carried him fireman style to the edge of the grave and tossed him in like a used towel after removing the gag and rope.

"Get back in the car honey."

She didn't reply, just sat their shaking and bawling.

"Let me help you baby, it's going to be alright."

I helped her to her feet, but she was in no condition to get herself there. I gently put her into the passenger seat and hugged her tightly, which only increased the intensity level of her howling.

I went back to the grave's edge. Chris was still unconscious, and although I wanted to see him suffer, it was time to get out of here as a result of Mary's condition. I squirted in some more gasoline and threw in another match.

"Feel the pain you evil prick," I said, as he ignited beside his barbequed partner in crime.

The smell of burning human tissue was causing me to gag. I grabbed the shovel from the car and hurriedly filled in the mattress and flesh packed hole.

As we made our way to the hotel, I couldn't help but feel that a huge burden had been lifted from my mind. Mary wasn't quite in check with me at the moment, but she'd come around.

19

On the Run

Maybe I was a sick bastard. It had been a full day since we'd burned those evil fuckers alive, and not one morsel of remorse had entered my head. I felt free as a bird, conscience as clear as a nun in church, and was invigorated like never before. The same couldn't be said for Mary. She was still a bag of nerves, flashbacks from the burning screams creating panic attacks like never before. She'd spent most of the time lying on the hotel room bed, unable to keep down any food, and any sleep she managed to grab was interrupted by the stark nightmare of our events, resulting in uncontrollable crying and irrepressible shaking. That's what I was here for though, to be the man, the rock in our relationship. I'd protect her with whatever means were necessary, and I was certain that anything that stood in our way would be a walk in the park compared to the destruction of Andrew and Chris.

I gently ran my fingers through her silky hair, and gazed lovingly at her new found outer beauty. I still couldn't get over the transformation. Any evidence of a cleft pallet was invisible to the naked eye, and now almost healed, her new lips were full and plump, and now screamed the words "blow job" every time I set eyes on them. I was guiltier about these thoughts than I was about the slaughter of the evil men, and decided it'd be best to keep them to myself.

I glanced in the mirror adjacent to the TV. I was looking great. My new appearance had really grown on me, especially with the added grey coloring. It may have put ten years on me, but I really suited it, besides anything was an improvement on the melted abortion of a face I'd had before. That was in the past now and I'd never have to stare at that again, or so I'd thought.

"HOLY CRAP," I said, blurting it out like an involuntary fart.

The old me was staring back at me like a possessed ghost from inside the TV screen, closely followed by Mary, deformed lip still intact. This was no dream, they were onto us. How we'd made the news was a mystery to me. I'd followed my plan to the letter, and was convinced it'd been as tight as a duck's ass under-water, but I was wrong.

My outburst snapped Mary out of her coma like existence, and my panic must've been evident.

"What's wrong Alexander," she trembled, with a look of terror invading her entire face.

"Shut up, shut up, they're onto us, they know it was us."

"How could they...."

"SHUT THE FUCK UP," I screamed. I felt awful for talking to her in such a foul way, but I had to hear the details. I needed to accelerate any plans, find out what they knew and how we could get ourselves out of a lifetime in prison. Mary remained silent as I turned up the TV and listened intently.

I used to be a real dog lover, but not anymore. Those fuckers had a sense of smell way beyond what any animal should ever possess. Much to my dismay, the bodies of Andrew and Chris had been discovered. The farmer who owned the field had been walking his dog earlier in the day and it had been sniffing around like crazy at the site of the execution. Even though the hole had been filled in, it was clear the previously grass covered area had been tampered with. The farmer prick must've called the cops and they'd discovered the bodies.

I needed to think, but it was virtually impossible as I was scared beyond belief, and Mary was now in a state of terror even worse than before. She remained quiet though, which helped slightly, but we had to get going to the airport *now*. I couldn't risk using my cell phone, as they were likely hoping they could track any calls we made. Luckily I paid the hotel in cash, so there was no tracing of any credit card usage either. We made it to the car on somewhat shaky legs and screeched off as quickly as possible. I'd gathered myself together a little better now and at least the cops believed they were looking for the old Alexander and Mary. I was amazed at how easily they'd got the identity of Andrew and Chris. Maybe they'd been in trouble with the law before and there were remnants of a couple of finger prints or perhaps dental records or something. That wasn't important right now, but how the fuck had they managed to get onto us so quickly?

20

Agent Royuc

"I need a full briefing on what your officers have found so far."

"Who the hell are you?" scowled the overweight Detective in charge, obviously no stranger to the donut shop's breakfast special.

"I'm Agent Wes Royuc, FBI."

His attitude changed, but from the frown remaining on his doughy face, he still wasn't over enthused by FBI involvement.

"Agent I'm Detective Jackson, we have reason to believe that both suspects are planning on escaping to Rio. Interrogation of the female suspect's work colleague, a Miss Monica Walker, revealed she received a call from Mary Elliott yesterday from a convenience store pay phone to say goodbye and that she would miss her, but as of today she would be gone. She never specified exactly where they were headed, but said they had to go where we couldn't get them and that it was only a short continent away."

"Good work detective. Did you get a track on the phone records?"

"Of course, we had officers down at the convenience store immediately, but so far no positive I.D's or any other useful information. We're pretty confident of Brazil though due to the extradition laws."

"OK Detective, great work. I'll be floating around the terminal here and will check back in with you shortly for an update."

*   *   *   *

Mary and I had no baggage to check in. It was to be a fresh start and no remnants of the past would accompany us on our trip. Now that we'd made it to the airport, I appeared as cool as a cucumber on the exterior, but my guts were churning inside like a fucking washing machine on super spin cycle. Mary looked as though she'd either seen a ghost or lightly powdered her face with some self-raising flour.

"It's going to be fine, just take a few deep breaths," I said rather unconvincingly. I wasn't sure if I really believed it myself, but if I lost it now, we were in big trouble. In light of recent terrorist activity, airport personnel were on the look out for suspicious behavior, and the last thing we needed was any unplanned interrogation.

"Hold my hand and I'll be OK."

I grasped her small, dainty fingers and could feel the tremor in her system. She gripped me tightly and I could almost feel her relax as we approached the check in desk. Hopefully the fake passports would pass the screening. They did look great though, and to the eye appeared as good as any genuine document. We were considerably early for the flight, but in light of our unplanned exposure, we didn't have many options.

"How many are checking in sir," asked the make-up caked girl on the counter.

"Just the two of us thanks," I said, ensuring I gave her a friendly smile. The more you embrace these folks, the less suspicion you arise.

"You're a little early for you flight sir, usually we don't check in anyone more than four hours before take-off."

"I told him we were leaving way too early," said Mary to the cosmetic coated lady. I was elated she'd calmed down and was adding some input to the conversation.

"Honey, we're only going for a couple of days, and I wanted to be sure we didn't miss the flight. You know what these roads are like with traffic, better early than late."

"That'll be a first. Usually he's just a typical man, never on time," said Mary, directing her reply to the young lady and shaking her head as she did do. The girl gave a pleasant chuckle.

"I can make an exception for you guys. Go grab yourselves a drink or a bite to eat or something. Do you have any bags to check in?"

"No it's only a brief visit. An old colleague of mine is getting married down there."

"Well I hope you have a wonderful time. Thanks again for flying with us."

She handed back our passports together with her beaming grin. I could have jumped the counter and gave her a huge kiss on the cheek, but I'd likely have left her with a deep nose print on her heavily encrusted face.

It wasn't quite over yet, we still had security to tackle, but we were getting close.

"Honey, you were fabulous there," I really meant the compliment.

"Thanks baby, I wasn't sure if I was doing the right thing or not, but I felt if I didn't say something then I was going to appear really edgy."

"Well you were superb. Listen, it's nearly over, just hang in there. Look, let's split up going through security. They're on the look out for a couple, so the less heat we can attract the better."

"OK honey, whatever you think."

"I'll meet you on the other side. No just go, we don't need any goodbye embraces before we head through here, that'll look really suspect."

"OK, love you."

"Love you to gorgeous."

She headed on her way and I ducked into the newsagent store and bought a magazine. I had no intention of reading it, but just wanted a reason to create a gap between us. I didn't want to just hang around and then follow. Security and police presence was also at an all time high from what I could see and it was no doubt in light of the recent newsflash. The airport was one of the first places they sent their resources.

I made my way to the security entrance and sailed through to the metal detector area after a quick flash of the new passport. I fucking hated this part. Take your shoes off, take you jacket off, laptops out of their cases and put in a separate tray. Blah, blah, fucking blah. At this rate we'd be stripping down to our underwear within ten years time. We can send a man to the moon, but can't create detection equipment that doesn't require taking off your shoes or the need for your laptop to be removed from its fucking bag.

There was no sign of Mary, which was either a good sign or she was camped out in some interrogation room.

I slipped off my shoes, took out my wallet and removed my watch. The turban wearing security officer waved me through the metal detector.

BEEP

What a shocker, I always set these things off.

"Please go back," said the Pakistani looking worker in a tone you wouldn't have used if addressing a dog. I was such a dick as I was still wearing a ring, but began to get a little frustrated as I couldn't remove it from my finger. The line behind me was becoming a little restless, but other than chopping the finger off, I was in a bit of a jam. Finally my dot headed friend grumpily waved me through, but made sure he covered every inch of my body with his hand held device, ensuring the only beep came from my finger. I was sure that deep down he'd been hoping for something in my pocket, so he could administer the rubber glove and lube treatment. He finally waved me on, but I had to resist every urge to make a wise remark to this power crazed towel head.

As I laced up my shoes I could see Mary hovering around the perfume store. We'd just hit the final turn.

"Hi honey, everything OK," I said, touching Mary on the shoulder as she looked into the store.

"God Alexander, you scared the shit outta me."

"Nothing to worry about right now, but there are cops everywhere today. They know we're in the building—I can feel it."

"Can I buy some perfume? I want to make sure I smell nice for you when we get to Rio."

"Sure. Let me get some cash out for you."

"It's OK, I can put it on my card."

The words caused me extreme disbelief, and it took me all my time not to fly into a rage and create a scene. Had the blonde hair completely rubbed off on her and impacted her brain.

"Your fucking card, your old credit card! Have you completely lost your mind? We make it past the check in desk, heightened security, and I now find out you're carrying a passport and credit card that don't match. Not to mention they're looking for the name of the woman that's clearly stamped on the fucking Mastercard tucked into your purse. If you use that they can track that shit you know. Is there anything else I should know about, like phone calls etc?"

I'd clearly upset her, but I was doing my best to keep it all together and she *was* jeopardizing our future together. Her head began to drop.

"I did make one call to Monica."

"I knew it, I just knew it. That's how they're here, they know we're here."

"I'm sorry Alexander, I'm really sorry. I just had to say goodbye to her. She's one of the only people who have always been there for me."

"It's OK sweetheart, I've been doing a couple of secretive things myself that I need to tell you about."

We found a seat and came clean on everything that had been going on, and finished it off with a strong hug.

I grabbed a couple of bags of chips and two diet cokes from the store, and brought them back to our seats. I finished off the bag and asked Mary to sneakily hand me her credit card. I slipped it David Blaine style into the empty wrapper, and disposed of it in the large flip top trash can, hopefully never to be seen again. We sat for a few hours, Mary falling asleep against me, but I was on edge. Police presence was only on the increase, and they were headed in the direction of our departure gate which was only a few hundred yards away. Surely there was no way they knew about our identity changes since the newscast earlier today. There was one way to find out, and it was going to be soon. Mary finally awakened, looking up at me with her half shut eyes and gave me a loving smile. I really loved her more than anything I'd ever loved before.

We made our way to the gate, keeping up the relaxed appearance as much as possible. The flight was beginning to board, and the line to get on the plane was enormous. An additional passport check had been enforced at the final possible place, and it wasn't the airline doing the checking, it was uniformed police. There were others standing around also, mingling with the people as they looked at the photographs in their hands, and attempting to match them up with a member of the crowd. I looked one of the officers in the eye. He glanced at the paper he was holding, then back at me, but continued on undeterred. It was clear now they had no idea of the identity switch. We neared the front of the line. I could even feel the warm air coming out of the approaching doorway. Then I saw him. I recognized one of the officers. Not the ones doing the passport checking, but another just a few feet away. He was engaged in conversation with one of the airline girls. Typical cop, two fugitives on the loose and he's more concerned about getting his fucking leg over. I kept my eye on him as we reached the front, and handed over our documents. His eyes never left her cleavage. The two officers politely handed us the passports back and told us to have a safe flight. It was more or less over now.

We took our seats in first class, John Power unaware of his complimentary gesture—for now anyway.

"Can I interest you in some pre-flight champagne?" said the ageing air hostess, in her overenthusiastic telephone voice. They were programmed to kiss the ass of first class passengers, but should've been trained to sound a little less robotic. Maybe she was a robot. It might have been the only thing keeping her upright. They certainly had relaxed the age policy for their profession over the years. Equal opportunity was a good thing, it had landed me my latest job after all, but at least grant the airline industry a waiver. Out went the compulsory tall, elegant looking young beauty, who smelled like the mixture of a cosmetic counter entwined with female sex juices. They were now few and far between, intermingled with the crusty old type, who smelled like a cocktail of worn shoes and asparagus tainted pee.

"We would love some champagne. Can you make the beautiful lady's a screwdriver please?"

Mary's face lit up like a Christmas tree, and her Angelina Jolie lips blew a kiss in my direction. Her new found looks now lined up like railway tracks with her inner persona.

Our glasses chimed together like a symphony with the sound of the aircraft doors closing. We were almost home free.

We taxied out of the terminal, heading for the runway. Our hands squeezed tighter and tighter together the further we went down the tarmac. The countdown to freedom had officially begun. We were off. The acceleration was even more stimulating than any previous take-off experience, and our spirits rose with the nose of the plane as we soared into the air. It was over and there was no going back.

"Well Agent Royuc, are you feeling as free as I am right now?" asked Mary.

"I feel wonderful gorgeous, and extremely satisfied. I feel like a super hero who's just eradicated the world from two evil villains."

"I know, it feels great," she said, smiling from ear to ear.

"Do you think they'll ever realize who Agent Wes Royuc really was back there?"

"They might, but they won't figure out the irony that Wes Royuc is an anagram for screw you."

"I might never have worked that out Agent Wes Royuc, or should I say Alexander McKenzie," whispered a voice from behind me. The familiarity of it sent a terrifying chill through my entire body—it was Detective Jackson.

"Well Alexander, let's talk about how we're going to get this plane back on the tarmac in the next five minutes, or the required amount of compensation you'll need to give me in order to bring on a sudden case of amnesia. It's your call."

978-0-595-42986-8
0-595-42986-6

Printed in the United States
74933LV00010B/171

9 780595 429868